"What are you doing?" Quinn asked, the merest hint of uncertainty in her eyes.

Ike said nothing. His expression remained somber, his body taut, exuding power and raw masculinity. Suddenly she whirled around, heading for the door. A firm grasp of her arm stayed her progress. It wasn't a move Ike had intended. Every move he made was measured and calculated, always controlled.

Yet less than five minutes alone with this fiery hellion and he was losing his cool. He began growing hotter not only under the collar, but in places farther down.

"Let go of my arm!"

He could feel her body shaking ever so slightly. Since her eyes were glaring daggers he assumed it was with rage. She surprised him by leaning forward, her lips precariously close to his. Dangerously close, even. "Let. Me. Go."

Their eyes locked. The room faded away. Time seemed to stop, too. She blinked. He followed the movement of her long lashes, felt his heart skip a beat. An inch, maybe less, and he could satisfy his curiosity on whether or not her lips were as soft as they appeared, or tasted as sweet. Like cotton candy, he imagined. One inch and…

Dear Reader,

There's something extra special about a person who succeeds against the odds. That's why it will be easy to cheer for Quinn, the heroine in this book. In hindsight, she reminds me of my mom, who after five children and twenty years as a psychiatric aide, decided to finish her degree and realize her dream of becoming a nurse (interrupted by marriage and the unexpected arrival of my oldest brother). In her fifties and sixties, she received a master's in social work and a BSN in nursing. She retired from mental health after thirty-five years, then spent another fifteen as a highly sought after and respected registered nurse.

The fact that she achieved her dreams showed me that I could, too. Hopefully this novel will inspire you. If Quinn can do it, you can do it.

One love…

Zuri

Sapphire ATTRACTION

ZURI DAY

ISBN-13: 978-0-373-86455-3

Sapphire Attraction

For questions and comments about the quality of this book please contact us at CustomerService@Harlequin.com.

HARLEQUIN®
™ www.Harlequin.com

Printed in U.S.A.

Zuri Day sneaked her first Harlequin romance at the age of twelve from her older sister's off-limits collection and was hooked from page one. Knights in shining armor and happily-ever-afters filled her teen years and spurred a lifelong love of reading. That she now creates these stories as a full-time, award-winning author is a dream come true! Splitting her time between the stunning Caribbean islands and Southern California, she's always busy writing her next novel. Zuri makes time to connect with readers and meet with book clubs. Contact her via Facebook (haveazuriday) or at zuri@zuriday.com.

Books by Zuri Day

Harlequin Kimani Romance

Diamond Dreams
Champagne Kisses
Platinum Promises
Solid Gold Seduction
Secret Silver Linings
Crystal Caress
Silken Embrace
Sapphire Attraction

Visit the Author Profile page at Harlequin.com for more titles.

Sometimes, when we try to control our feelings,
We meet someone who sends our heart and mind reeling.
Life becomes dimmer, no true satisfaction,
Until we give in to the fire-hot attraction.

Chapter 1

The smooth sounds of classic jazz filled the four-door luxury sedan. Ike Drake Jr. had had a stressful weekend, and he appreciated the way Wes Montgomery's fluid guitar licks poured over his soul like water, washing the frenzy away.

In his preteen years, Ike had temporarily eschewed the music his grandfather loved in favor of the pop and hip-hop stars who then provided the soundtrack of his life. That didn't last long. By tenth grade, during summers spent on Walter Drake's farm, he regained an appreciation for his elder's favorite musicians: Miles, Ramsey, Dizzy, Charlie and Wes. He also shared Walter's passion for fishing, golf and classic cars like the meticulously restored 1961 Ferrari Spider he now drove. His grandmother Claire had labeled him an old soul since childhood, and even way back then had affectionately called him Mr. Ike.

Ike tapped a beat on his steering wheel, focused on the music and tried to forget about why his jaws were tight and his muscles were in knots. Days of Paradise, an annual event celebrating the incorporation of Paradise Cove and held during Labor Day weekend, was always a hectic time. The Drakes were among the town's founding families, along with one of the wealthiest and most well-known. Their company, Drake Realty Plus, had built and/or sold many of the homes and apartments in which citizens resided. Ike's brother Niko was mayor of the city. The Drake family participation was high profile and taxing. In addition to serving as the grand marshal for this year's parade, he was on the Days of Paradise board and had helped oversee a three-day carnival and annual charity ball. These extracurricular activities on top of being immersed in the closing of a deal costing more than a hundred million dollars brought enough anxiety to raise his blood pressure. No one would fault him for being stressed and on edge. But if he was honest with himself, he'd admit that all of these very important issues weren't the real reason for his discomfort.

The real reason was a woman named Quinn.

She'd burst into his world on Saturday night at the fundraiser ball. Like a tornado, she'd bowled over everyone in her path and left hearts and emotions strewn around the room. Ike's were among them.

The soothing sound of Wes's "Bumping on Sunset" gave way to the memories of Saturday night. Without realizing it, his relaxed shoulders tensed. He gripped the wheel.

"Who's that?"

Ike and two of his brothers, Warren and Niko, stood near the main bar in the Paradise Cove Country Club's ballroom. Their position afforded an unobstructed view of the room's entrance, through which a sexy siren who had elicited Niko Drake's question had just entered.

"I don't know," Warren responded, his eyes glued to the room's sudden star attraction as he sipped a neat bourbon. "But I guarantee she won't remain anonymous for long."

Ike could only stare. The stranger was stunning. Tall, he imagined around five-seven, but appearing statuesque because of strappy stiletto sandals and a high ponytail that exposed dainty drop earrings and an elegant long neck. Her dress was ultraclassic—a sleeveless black gown with a gently scooped neckline that hugged her slender body to the knee before flaring out into a dramatic train. Ike subconsciously nodded his approval as she came farther into the room, looking neither left nor right but either straight ahead or down at the petite satin-clad woman beside her. Classy, conservative, elegant...a perfect fit in this country-club crowd. Her mannerisms were understated, and while he was sure she was aware of her beauty and the subtle murmur of voices that followed in her wake, she seemed admirably unaffected.

After a long on-again, off-again relationship with a woman who, like him, had grown up in PC, Ike was single. Were he looking for a wife, she could potentially be a candidate. She was someone he decided to meet before the night was over. His eyes followed her as she passed the brothers, several feet away but partially hidden. His interest grew as he took in her regal bearing. He smiled as she passed them. But when he saw the back of her gown, his expression changed. He became as annoyed as he was attracted.

WTH?

The back of her Chai original was as risqué as the front was moderate. It plunged from her shoulders to just above her backside, exposing an expanse of creamy, smooth skin that made him think of vanilla ice cream covered with cashews and warm caramel. The back of the dress was made of lace, with carefully placed flowers in the fabric the only thing that allowed the enchantress to maintain any modesty at all. It was way too revealing, Ike noted. He now clearly understood why her entrance had caused the crowd to murmur, women to narrow their eyes and men to get poked in the side for staring. The woman was practically nude.

"Careful, darling. Scowling too hard for too long may cause permanent wrinkles."

Ike had been so intent on watching—some would say judging—the room's star attraction that he hadn't even seen his date approach. "Did you see that? What a spectacle!" When the woman disappeared amid the throng crowding the bar, Ike finally managed to tear his eyes away. "The way she's dressed is disrespectful. I can't believe Mrs. Newman didn't insist she change before bringing her here."

Audrey Ross knew Ike well and quietly noted his strong reaction to the new girl in town. She had been his on-again, off-again girlfriend for the past ten years. They were no longer dating but remained good friends.

Niko had walked away but Warren remained. He turned to Audrey. "Is she related to her?"

"Maggie Newman?"

"Yeah."

Audrey nodded. "Her granddaughter, Quinn Taylor."

"I don't remember seeing her before," Ike said. "And the way she grabbed everyone's attention, most folks in this town haven't, either."

Quinn emerged from the bar area with two glasses of champagne and carried them over to where Maggie Newman sat. Ike forced himself to quit looking, but Warren continued to enjoy the show. Almost every eligible bachelor seemed to vie for her attention as she calmly held court at one of the room's center tables, the one next to the table occupied by the Drakes.

Once again, Audrey was a fountain of information. "She grew up on the East Coast and attended an elite boarding school in Switzerland before returning to America to get her college degree. At some point she got engaged to a prince, then broke things off mere weeks before the wedding. That happened recently—just a few months ago. It caused a minor scandal, as you can imagine. One of many she's created since her teen years. Glen finally had enough."

Ike's head snapped around. "Glen Taylor? The judge?" Audrey nodded. "What could he possibly have to do with her?"

"Believe it or not, he's her dad."

"The conservative Republican? I don't believe it."

"It's true."

"Where's her mother?"

"That's a mystery," Audrey mused. "No one knows about her, what happened to their marriage or why Quinn was raised by her dad."

"I'm surprised anything about her got by you, Audrey," Warren said. "How do you know so much?"

"Mom and Mrs. Newman are sorors, and good friends. I happened to be there during their afternoon-tea chat, shortly after Quinn came to town. At any rate, the judge arrived on the West Coast as a single father and from what I hear, never mentioned Quinn's mother or any other woman from his past. The closest she had to a mother figure was her grandmother and a nanny, who was obviously long on patience and short on discipline. The result was a spoiled brat who grew into a troublemaking teen. Shortly after his marriage to San Francisco socialite Viviana Lange, Quinn was shipped overseas. Knowing the Langes and their obsession with image, that doesn't surprise me. The story from there is public knowledge, as it's been largely played out in the society pages of the *Chronicle.*" She took a sip from her wineglass, watching Quinn's deft handling of her admirers. "From the look of things," Audrey finished, "she's still a troublemaker."

"I wonder what she's doing here," Ike muttered, thinking out loud.

Audrey waved at an associate, talking over her shoulder as she walked away. "If the past continues to repeat itself, we'll no doubt find out."

The scowl returned as Ike pondered what Andrey had shared. Glen Taylor was a successful and well-respected judge. Both avid golfers, they'd run into each other on a course or two, the first time at the country club where they were now. Ike liked Glen and respected Mrs. Newman. He doubted either feeling would apply to the woman named Quinn.

Later on, this thought gained traction. When Quinn was introduced to his family, Ike didn't like that she addressed his mother by her first name, or her flirty nature when meeting him and his brothers. More than once during the formal dinner, the quiet was interrupted by her raucous laughter as she sat at a table surrounded by men. When he saw her leave with one of the town's notorious playboys instead of Mrs. Newman, with whom she'd come, that bothered him, too. He told himself it didn't. But it did.

A roaring engine mixed with a pounding bass brought Ike out of his reverie. He looked to his left, saw a driver speeding like a bat out of Hades and had just enough time to accelerate and sharply turn the steering wheel in an effort to avoid the car as it crossed the center line. The head-on collision was prevented but a crash was not. Metal crunched against metal. Ike's car jumped the curb and struck a mailbox. The force introduced his forehead to the steering wheel, a meeting that rendered him senseless. He smelled burned rubber and shook his head to clear the cloudiness. Wrong move. Instead of clearing, his head began pounding, even as he heard voices and someone yelling to call 9-1-1. He looked over to see the car that had hit him, a fiery red Corvette with loud music still blasting. The driver's head rested against the seat. Blood dripped from a nasty cut. It was the troublemaker Quinn Taylor, wreaking havoc again.

Chapter 2

"Are you okay?"

When he went against the advice of the bystanders—one of whom was an off-duty EMT—and got out of his car to confront Quinn, that was not the question Ike had intended to ask. "Are you crazy?", "What in the heck were you doing?" or "Why did you swerve into my lane?" was more like what he had in mind. But when he reached the driver's side door, looked into frightened hazel-brown eyes partially hidden by naturally long lashes and took in the quivering lips sporting pale pink gloss, Quinn's well-being suddenly became important than a verbal confrontation.

"I'm sorry. The dog. Did you see him? Jumped right in front of my car..." Quiet replaced chaos as she killed the engine and with it the blaring music. The movement caused blood to drip from the cut on the side of her head onto her arm. "Oh, my God, I'm bleeding!" She snatched the rear-view mirror toward her and glimpsed an ugly gash on her temple just as an ambulance siren announced its approach.

"You were driving like a..." Ike managed before becoming distracted by the same tempting flesh that had stayed on his mind long after the charity ball was over, which meant far longer than he should have allowed. He assumed Quinn wore shorts, but from his position couldn't quite tell. All he could see were bare legs that seemed to go on forever and hardened, pert nipples pressed against a ripped tee. "Way too fast," he finished, almost as an afterthought.

"I was driving just fine," she retorted with a pout. "It was the dog. Did you see…" She looked around, then back into Ike's accusing gaze. "I swear, a dog ran in front of my car!"

"Blaming this on a dog, huh?" He looked around, becoming more irritated by the second. His smashed-up pride and joy being only one of several reasons. "Where is it now?"

"Good God, man! Are you all right?"

Ike turned toward the familiar voice behind him. His focus went from the look of horror on Warren's face to where his eyes traveled after asking the question. Ike had only glanced at the Ferrari's front end. He wasn't ready to see the side that had taken the brunt of the collision. Didn't want to confirm what he already knew to be true, that rare and expensive car parts had been damaged. Didn't want to believe that his prized 250, one of only thirty-six such models ever made, driven in public fewer than two or three times a year, had crossed paths with a Corvette-driving Andretti wannabe using a street in the town square as her racetrack.

"Don't even say it," he warned Warren, a hand up as if to ward off the painful truth. "It's bad, I know."

"What happened?"

"Reckless driving," he answered with a nod toward Quinn.

"I was not driving recklessly. I tried to dodge an animal."

"A phantom dog," Ike added, a heavy dose of sarcasm served on the side.

Quinn's comeback was interrupted by EMTs rushing to her car. "Excuse me, guys," the woman said, her tone businesslike but not unfriendly. "We need to get to her."

The men stepped back. Ike turned toward his car. The quick movement made him dizzy. He stumbled.

"Whoa, watch out, brother." Warren jumped to his side. "You probably shouldn't be standing. Let me get one of those guys over here."

Ike waved a dismissive hand. "I'm fine."

"You think you are, but there may be internal injuries."

"There are definitely external ones," he said through gritted teeth as he crossed back over to his wrecked car.

Steeling himself, he walked around it. The meticulous paint job that had taken months to complete now covered a misaligned and bent hood, caved-in side door and hanging fender. His jaw clenched in anger. Accidents happened, a fact of life. But this one could easily have been avoided. Even if a dog had crossed the street—an excuse that he found suspect, since he saw no dog in sight—there would have been more control and time to act if she hadn't been speeding. Her actions were reckless, her reaction less than responsible or contrite. Of all the Drake brothers, Ike was normally the calmest, most calculating and even-keeled. But with the exhausting weekend, the pressure of closing the San Francisco deal and now a senseless accident in his prized Ferrari, Ike was ready to explode.

Warren walked over and stood next to his brother. "I'm sorry, man. I know how long it took to get it in mint condition."

"Interesting how you're apologizing while all she talked about was a dog in the street."

"It could have been worse."

"Yeah, she could have been driving a tank. I just don't—" Ike stopped short, his expression incredulous. "Did you hear that BS?" Instead of waiting for an answer, Ike walked over to where a police officer had joined the EMT team checking out Quinn's injuries.

"...I think he was, but I'm not sure," Quinn finished, her voice weak and body sagging as the medical personnel attended to her cuts and bruises. "I feel woozy. I can't..."

One of the EMTs spoke up. "Officer, we need to get her to the hospital."

"Not before I clear up her fuzzy uncertainty," Ike butted in, bristling at an act he thought might win Quinn an Academy Award but no sympathy from him. "The accident was her fault, one hundred percent."

Ike had addressed the officer, but his eyes stayed glued on Quinn. They'd wrapped bandages around her head and were treating the ugly gash near her temple. A medic shone a penlight into her eyes as they wheeled her away.

"What happened?"

"She said a dog jumped in front of her, but she was going too fast—slammed into me before I could react."

The officer looked around. "Did you see it?"

"Nope."

"All right, sir. Wait here so I can take your statement. I need to get her information before they take off."

Warren came over. "Ike, I know you're upset. But remember what Audrey said the other night about the judge being her father. I'm sure they've got the type of insurance to handle this, and if not, the judge has the cash."

"It's definitely going to get handled. She is going to pay for the restoration and any other charges that are incurred as a result of her recklessness."

Warren looked over as the ambulance drove away. "Both of your cars are damaged. But it looks like the two of you are lucky to come out of this with only minor injuries."

Even angry, Ike's heart hitched at the sight of her being wheeled into the back of the van. "Yes, I'm grateful for that. And even though she's a hellion, I hope Quinn is okay."

Warren's brow raised at the unexpected tenderness he heard in his brother's voice. "What about you, man? How are you?"

It was the first time Ike had given any thought to his own body and possible injuries. He flexed his shoulders, raised and lowered his arms, and moved his head from side to side. "Other than being sore as all get-out tomorrow, I guess I'll live."

Just then, one of the medics who'd been working on Quinn walked over to where Warren and Ike stood. He looked at Ike. "Were you the one in the accident, sir?"

"Yes."

"Mind if we check you out?"

"No need for that. I'm fine."

"You may feel fine now, but later, after the adrenaline stops and the shock wears off, the pain might come."

"If that happens, I'll call my doctor." The medic nodded and left. The police officer rejoined Ike, with Warren beside them. "Okay, sir. I need your driver's license, registration and proof of insurance."

Ike retrieved the items and handed them over.

The officer recorded the information and returned the papers. "Want to tell me your side of how this accident occurred?"

"I was driving down the street, no problems, no traffic. Reached the corner, stopped and began driving through the intersection. Next thing I know I'm swerving to avoid a speeding car suddenly in my lane. Barely had time to react before she'd crashed into me."

"Did she acknowledge that she was speeding?"

"Are you kidding? She didn't even acknowledge she ran into me and not vice versa. Blamed it on a dog that's conveniently disappeared, and even if it had been present, it wouldn't have posed the same kind of problem for someone driving the speed limit."

Ike watched the officer jot down notes. "What did she say?"

The officer spoke without looking up. "She said speed had nothing to do with the accident. As you just stated, she mentioned the dog."

"Doesn't surprise me that she'd try and skirt responsibility for this. But you ticketed her, right?"

"Didn't get the chance. The medics feared a concussion and wanted to get her to the hospital as soon as possible. That's necessary so that a more serious injury can be ruled out."

"But she is going to receive a citation, correct? I don't

want her getting away with this, and I definitely want her held accountable for all repair costs."

The officer looked at the wrecked classic. "That's got to hurt," he acknowledged with a shake of his head. "What is that, a Chevy?"

Not a comment to normally make one want to punch a guy, but at the moment that's how Ike felt. Warren's chuckle compounded his anger. Thankfully it also diverted his mind from going fisticuffs, which Ike had never done in his life. The stress, no doubt, had allowed the uncharacteristic thought to surface, even momentarily. It wasn't illegal not to be a car enthusiast. Of course, one couldn't go to jail for not answering a stupid question, either.

"How is this going to be handled?" he asked instead.

"Well, I'm going to take a look around and investigate the scene, find out if there are any other witnesses and turn in a report based on those findings. If you ask me, though, worse things can happen than to get tangled up with a pretty little thing like the gal driving that Corvette. Who knows, she might be open to some kind of...negotiation. Know what I mean?"

"No, Officer Morris," Ike said, crossing his arms as he checked the young man's badge. "Why don't you explain it to me exactly?"

Officer Morris suddenly became very interested in the fine print of the report he held in his hand as a healthy shade of red crept from his neck to his chin.

"I suggest your investigation of this accident be a thorough and accurate one, because I'm going to contact a good friend who happens to be chief of police and ask him to take a personal interest in this matter and ensure that justice is served."

"Will do, Mister—" Officer Morris looked down at the paper "—Drake. Um, right. I'll be sure to take witness statements and record everything as accurately as possible."

"You do that. And keep me posted on the outcome. I'm

not letting her off the hook for this. Having no consequences for past rash actions is probably why she's so careless today."

By now tow trucks were on the scene. Ike walked over to the driver closest to his car and gave him a card to the garage where his car had been restored. "Be very careful," he warned the freckle-faced young man. "As damaged as it is, that car is still my baby."

The two brothers turned toward where Warren's truck was parked. "Are you sure you're all right?"

Ike nodded. "I'm fine."

They reached the truck and got inside. "Where to?" Warren asked his brother.

Ike looked at his watch. "Home, I guess. There aren't any other meetings scheduled or urgent business matters at the office, so I may just as well work from there." For a minute they rode in silence. "What were you doing away from the office?"

"I wrapped up work early and was headed home for the day. Charli's been getting on me about increasing my daddy duties and helping out more. I told her to get a nanny, but she refuses. Says nobody else is going to tell her daughter what to do."

"Did you ask if that included you?"

"No, but I probably should." The brothers laughed. "She's an amazing wife and a fantastic mother, but a little overprotective. And speaking of which, you know when Mom finds out about this she's going to want you checked out."

"I'll call my doctor and, if he thinks it necessary, have him stop by."

"Good idea. Though I'm sure that seeing your Ferrari smashed up hurt worse than any physical injury would."

Warren, three years younger than Ike and a lot like their grandfather Walter, was the only other brother who had an appreciation for classic cars.

"Man, you know it. I just got every detail back to its original state, what, maybe a month or so ago? It took us forever to find that particular siding. And then a careless driver had to go and smash right into it."

"I'm sure it was an accident, not intentional."

"Accident or not, it happened because she was driving too fast, and probably distracted by the loud music blaring from her car stereo. Heck, she may have even been texting."

"You don't know that."

"No, I don't. But I wouldn't doubt it."

"And even with that possibility, you're still concerned about her welfare."

Ike's head quickly turned toward his brother. "Says who?"

"Says you. Back there."

"I said no such thing."

"When she was being wheeled into the ambulance. You said you hoped she was okay."

"I don't remember saying that."

"And you couldn't take your eyes off her. Didn't even know how badly your car was damaged until I got there."

"I don't remember that, either."

Warren gave his brother a lopsided grin. "Well, I was standing right next to you, bro, and you were definitely checking her out." They reached the gated entrance to the Golden Gates community where several Drake family members lived. Ike lived just a couple blocks over from his parents, and Niko, two years younger than Ike, lived a mere block away. Warren tapped a device on his dash and the gates opened. "No one can fault you for being concerned about Quinn. She's gorgeous, smart..."

"Spoiled, irresponsible, ill-mannered. So don't even start."

"Start what?"

"Whatever you're preparing to instigate by blowing up a general statement made when my brain was scrambled."

"Ha! Oh, so now the comment that you don't remember making was said while you weren't in your right mind."

"Correct."

Warren laughed again. "Okay, you go ahead and believe that. I don't know why you're fighting it. If I weren't married, I'd probably ask her out."

"Could you see someone like her feeling at home on your ranch? No, I don't think that would have been a match. She's more Terrell or Julian's speed, and closer to their ages."

"How old do you think she is?"

"Too young for me."

Warren gave a disgruntled grunt. "I bet she's not ten years younger than you—probably more like five."

"She could be five years older than me chronologically and still too young. Or perhaps I should have said immature."

"You're full of it, Ike. There's no way you can sit there and tell me you don't find Quinn attractive."

"She's gorgeous, no doubt. Just not the type of woman I'm looking for."

They reached Ike's house. Warren pulled into his driveway and turned off the truck's engine.

"So you are looking. That means you and Audrey are still off again?"

"Audrey and I are off forever."

"I'll believe that when I see it."

"No, it's for real this time. She agrees, too. Said that after ten years I should know if she's the one. Plus, she's not getting any younger and wants kids. She needs to be with someone ready to commit."

"And that's not you?"

"Doesn't look like it," Ike said with a sigh. "And to tell you the truth, I don't know why. She has all the qualities I'd want in a wife. Everything except that spark, that something that leaves no doubt that you'd lay down your life for that woman. Like what I see between our grandparents, between Mom and Dad, heck, even between you and Charli, Niko and Monique, and Teresa and Atka. But it's not there.

I couldn't lie to her and say it was, nor could I lie and say a commitment was imminent. So, yes, it's officially and completely over, but we parted as friends."

He opened his door. "Thanks for the lift, Warren. I'd tell you not to share the accident with Mother, but she probably knows already." As if on cue, his cell phone rang. He pulled it out and showed Warren the picture of their smiling mother, indicating that she was indeed the caller. "See what I mean?"

He waved to his brother as he walked up the steps to his front door, placing the phone beneath his ear as he let himself in. "Yes, I was in an accident, Mom, and no, I'm not hurt," he said in greeting.

"I know all that," Jennifer answered. "I'm calling to inquire as to whether or not you've called to check on Quinn, and to know what type of flowers you had sent to her room."

Chapter 3

Ike actually pulled the phone away from his ear to see if the image had changed. Where was his mother and who was this stranger asking the ridiculous question? "You're joking, right?"

"Why would I joke about performing a classy, kind act?"

"Obviously because you don't know as much about the accident as you think you do." Ike bypassed his living/dining area and went into the kitchen. He pulled a bottle of water from the fridge then continued to his office. "The accident was totally Quinn's fault, one that save for her negligence could have been avoided."

"Be that as it may, you seem to be fine and she's in the hospital, where she'll be overnight for observation. So the gentlemanly thing to do is to send flowers and a card wishing her a speedy recovery."

"All I plan on sending her is a repair bill, and that through my lawyer."

Jennifer tsked. "Ike Anthony Drake, do not speak that way. It's not how you were raised. I understand you being upset and can only imagine how bad you feel that your car was damaged. But it's just a car, Ike, not a life. That neither of you were seriously injured is a blessing. Now, would you like for me to handle that for you, dear, or will you have your assistant send them in the morning first thing?"

Ike was dumbfounded into silence.

"Something grand and cheery, I'm thinking," Jennifer continued in the silence. "Bird-of-paradise, red ginger and lilies—no blemishes, of course. And orchids, for their lovely scent. Purple would be nice. All accented with tall palm leaves and—"

"Mom. Excuse me for interrupting, but…I'll take care of everything."

And he would. That his idea of everything had not included a delivery of flowers to the woman who'd crashed into his Ferrari was something he saw no benefit in sharing.

"Sorry to prattle, darling. You know how much I love flowers. And so does your father. After almost four decades of marriage, he still brings them to me every week. Gets them from the florist shop in the town square."

"He's your husband. I'm the victim. So forgive me for not seeing a connection."

"Oh, sweetheart. You've always been the serious son. At least until Julian was born. Among our children, you two are the most alike. Both of you can stand to lighten up a bit and not always take life so seriously. Except when it comes to your health. I understand you refused one at the scene, but have you seen a doctor?"

"Jeez, Mom, how do you get this information so quickly?"

"It's a strategic process, darling, honed over time and not easily or readily explained. But very handy when one has six rambunctious sons."

"Don't leave the rambunctious sister out."

"Unlike Teresa, the sensible sister, I admit London can sometimes be a bit unruly. But that comes from an inner excitement and zest for life."

"No, it comes from being Daddy's baby girl, led to believe that the sun revolves around her."

"We may have been too lenient in those early years, that's true. But your little sister has grown into an amazing woman. You know, the young lady in the accident, Quinn Taylor, reminds me somewhat of her."

"Now that's a connection easily recognized. Quinn's a spoiled brat, too."

"She's also very beautiful and full of life. At the ball, I found her delightful."

"I found her irritating, and my opinion of her has only plummeted from there."

"Hmm, interesting." She paused. "Well, dear, do see a doctor. Your father was in an accident once and refused medical treatment because he thought he was fine. It took five years for what was then a slight sprain to show up as pain in his lower back. Minor surgery was required to fix what could have been handled through a chiropractor if caught in time."

"Definitely wouldn't want that to happen. I'll call him now. Bye, Mom."

Ike left a message with his physician's assistant and then called Niko. When he wasn't in the mayor's office, Ike tried his cell.

"What's up, Ike?"

"A little situation I want to run past you. Tried your office phone. Where are you?"

"Temecula."

"That's right. I'd forgotten all about your getaway with Monique. I'm sorry to bother you."

"No bother at all. In fact, your timing is perfect. Monique is at the spa, bonding with her cousin-in-law and sister-in-law."

"Diamond and who else, Faye or Marissa?"

"Marissa."

"Where's Faye?"

"Working too hard, like most doctors."

"It's nice that your wife is spending quality time with that side of the family. How's everybody else doing?"

Niko filled Ike in on the latest happenings with their Southern California cousins who owned and operated Drake Wines & Resort, an award-winning five-star resort in Southern California's wine country.

"So we're happy to let them have their pamper day," Niko

finished. "Because come tomorrow night it's the husbands' turn—me, Jackson, Donovan and floor seats at Staples."

"Floor seats? Must have cost you a fortune."

"Jackson has connections with a big-time sports agent, Michael Morgan. The tickets came from him."

"Now that's what I call a connection. Does he have an extra?"

"Afraid not."

"Then thanks for letting me know about floor seats at a game I can't attend."

"You're welcome." The brothers laughed. "So why'd you call?"

"I was in an accident today and need some legal advice."

"Are you okay?"

"Banged up, but I'll live. The other driver was taken to the hospital for observation, but from the looks of everything she'll be fine."

"She?"

"Yes."

"Who?"

"Quinn Taylor."

"Damn. Lucky you."

"Right. Lucky me."

"I didn't mean that sarcastically. That is one gorgeous lady. Running into her might turn out to be the best thing that ever happened to you."

"I highly doubt that. And she ran into me."

"What happened?" Ike told him. "If it's a situation that's clearly her fault, more than likely her insurance will cover the damages. So why do you need a lawyer?"

"One, because no matter how good her insurance, it will likely not cover the costs of replacing the parts that will have to be fixed. They are rare and expensive."

"Aw, man! She wrecked the Ferrari."

"Now you're getting there, brother. Feel my pain."

"I feel it. You just got that baby in mint condition." Niko

whistled. "You're right. That bill is likely to run over and above what her policy covers."

"Exactly. Which brings me to the second reason I need legal advice—to prosecute her for reckless endangerment."

"I thought you said this was an accident."

"One caused by her using our streets as a racetrack."

"Yes, Ike, but accidents happen. Give it twenty-four to forty-eight hours before setting anything in motion. The situation is likely to look quite different once you stop aching and cool down."

"I'm angry, Niko, not irrational, and will not change my mind. This accident was a direct result of her foolishness. Her beauty isn't going to sway me from making her face the consequences. It's time she learned a lesson on cause and effect."

"I'd think you'd want to school her in some…less combative areas."

"Not you, too. First it was the police wanting to go easy, then Mom wanting me to send flowers and now you're suggesting I make a date with that daredevil? That would hardly be practical. She's much too wild."

"Which would make taming her all the more satisfying."

"You're suggesting that I court her when why I called you is to take her to court. So your unrequested yet respected personal opinion aside, legally, how do I proceed?"

Niko laughed. "All right, man. I hear you. But I can't help you, not directly. My expertise is corporate law. You need an accident and personal injury attorney."

"Do you know any?"

"Not offhand, but let me make a couple calls and get back with you. Meanwhile, follow Mom's advice and send those flowers. It's the right thing to do."

Later, Niko referred Ike to an attorney who was not only well versed in the field but quick to act. Two days after the accident, attorney Lance Holden demanded the police report be completed and filed. The day after that, Quinn was charged with reckless driving. A week later, Lance represented Ike at an arraignment at which Quinn pled not guilty. Lance then suggested they avoid a trial by requesting a pretrial conference in the judge's chambers. That was fine with Ike. His demand for repayment and appropriate punishment would be met. Victory was all but assured. According to Lance, the matter would be resolved shortly. The defense attorney had left court, heading to his office and a meeting with Quinn.

Chapter 4

Quinn sat and seethed. Was she really sitting in a lawyer's office over a car accident? Seriously?

"Where is he?" She stared at the door as if it had an answer.

"I'm sure he'll be here shortly, Kristin Quinn. Try and stay calm."

On cue, the door opened. A harried-looking lawyer in a wrinkled suit charged into the room, carrying a bulging briefcase in one hand and a coffee mug in the other.

"Hello, ladies. Sorry to have kept you waiting. A case ran late." He set the briefcase and travel mug on the desk, then extended his hand to Quinn. "I'm Joey Wang, the defense attorney who'll be handling this case."

Quinn's handshake was as lackluster as her desire to be here.

He shook Maggie's hand as well. As he walked behind his desk she said, "We hope you were able to do what the other attorney couldn't."

"I'm afraid that's not why I called you here. The victim is adamant. He wants this matter to be handled in court."

"I can't stand that man! He's such a jerk!" A hearty stiletto-heeled foot stomp was the exclamation point to her anger.

"Quinn, please." Maggie reached over and patted Quinn's hand. "Take a breath."

Quinn did as instructed even as she gave the attorney an icy stare.

Maggie looked at the attorney. His bewildered face matched her own.

"I understand you being upset, Ms. Taylor. These types of cases are often settled out of court. But I assure you that this case will be handled with the utmost care, and in a way that makes this unfortunate situation as easy as possible. Which is why I brought you here." He looked at Quinn. "It's to recommend that you change your plea."

"To guilty? No way."

"Given the preponderance of evidence, which includes witness statements, a guilty plea can possibly assist in resolving this matter quickly."

"You're asking me to plead guilty even though the accident wasn't my fault," Quinn insisted.

"What's the difference?" Maggie asked.

"Guilty means that one admits responsibility, that they are at fault. When this happens, the sentence—or in this case whatever reprimand the judge would impose, since jail is unlikely—would be lighter than what a jury typically hands down. 'No contest' means that the defendant agrees to the facts presented but not to their guilt in what happened as a result."

Quinn's ears perked up. "Meaning I wouldn't be liable for his car damage?"

"No, that is not what I mean. The eyewitness testimony and police investigation both point to you being at fault. His repairs will be your responsibility no matter how you plead. Then there is the matter of your driving history and the number of speeding tickets you've received in the past five years."

Quinn's shoulders slumped. There was no arguing with that truth.

"This will be classified as a misdemeanor. You'll likely get off with a fine, some type of community service and a suspended license for no more than ninety days. If you slow down and go the next few years without additional tickets, you could approach the judge to have the charge expunged from your record."

"Unacceptable," Quinn said with her back ramrod straight. "Grandmother, can we talk about this privately, please?"

"What's there to talk about, Quinn? You did hit the young man's car."

"Isn't that what insurance is for?"

"I'm afraid these expenses are going to go beyond whatever policy you have," Joey replied. "When fully restored and in pristine condition, cars like the one you hit sell for half a million bucks."

Quinn huffed in disbelief. "That's ridiculous."

Maggie raised a hand to her chest. "Oh, good Lord."

"The '61 Ferrari is a prized classic. Few were made and most of those are in various states of disrepair. That makes the one you wrecked even more valuable, and leads to the final point."

"There's more?" Quinn asked.

Joey answered while opening his briefcase and pulling out a manila envelope. "The owner of the Ferrari has decided not to wait until after the trial to take additional action. He has filed suit against you, Quinn, to ensure the repairs will be handled."

Quinn eyed her grandmother. "Sued me! Can you believe it? Should I still not be upset?"

Instead of answering the question, Maggie addressed the attorney. "Mister, um…"

"Wang, ma'am. But please, call me Joey."

"Joey, thank you so much for all you've done. I'll discuss this with my granddaughter and get back with you shortly."

"As soon as possible, please. The victim and his attorney want this matter resolved in all due haste."

They'd not taken two steps outside before Quinn started in. "Grandmother, please talk to Dad again. One phone call and this would go away! I don't know why he's being so stubborn!"

"One could say the same for you," Maggie answered, with kind eyes.

"Me? Okay, maybe you're right. Even though there was a very good reason for me to swerve, I did in fact hit the other car. So I'll pay the fine and fix his stupid car. But community service? There's no way. And with Trent coming to town next week, a suspended license is totally out of the question."

Trent Corrigan was Quinn's plus one when she needed one, a mood lifter with a great gift of gab. She called him Trench Coat. He called her Q-Tip. They'd been best friends since high school.

"I was talking about the strained relationship between you and your father, the animosity that's been present since he remarried. That happened twelve years ago, honey, when you were thirteen. How long are you going to hold on to the anger of your youth?"

"I don't see him making a move to repair things, either."

They reached the car and got inside. Maggie turned toward Quinn, grasped her hands and squeezed softly. "Quinn, my dear. I love you so very much. The attitude you're exhibiting is partly my fault. I shouldn't have spoiled you, but those beautiful hazel-brown eyes would get me every time.

"Your father isn't perfect. But there's one thing I know for sure, and it's that he loves you. Are there other ways he can show it besides the ones he's tried? Certainly. But like you, honey, he's doing the best he can."

"Grandmother—"

"No, no need for a counterargument. You have to handle life on your own terms. As for spoiling you, I don't regret a single one of the all too few days we shared when you were younger." Maggie ran a hand along Quinn's cheek. "You missed so much. Your mother gone and your dad always so busy with work."

"Work and Viviana. Don't leave her out."

"And his wife, yes. I tried to fill the void in ways that may not have served you. There were too few rules and almost no consequences. All things considered, what the young man is asking is not beyond the pale."

Quinn started the car and headed home, careful to observe the speed limit along the way.

"Is that why Dad is refusing to help me? To teach me another lesson?"

"I can't answer that, dear. But regarding the pretrial conference, I agree with Joey. This matter will be settled through the court. There's no getting out of that. Changing your plea seems the best thing to do."

Quinn didn't voice the reaction she felt. *We'll see.*

They arrived home, but Quinn's plans weren't to stay long. She went upstairs and returned with her jacket.

"Going out again?"

"For a bit. While I still have a license."

"Do be careful, darling."

Quinn jumped into the rental Corvette she'd been given while her own was being repaired. She would have liked nothing more than to rev the V-6 engine and use major horsepower to take the car from zero to sixty in a little under four seconds flat. She resisted the temptation. Took her time to gain a cool head. Talking Ike Drake into standing down on his notion of justice would take all the charm and calm persuasion she possessed.

Halfway to Drake Realty, her cell phone rang. She tapped the phone icon on the steering wheel to answer the call from her lone PC friend, whom she'd met the first time on a visit at the age of twelve. "Hey, Peyton."

"What are you doing?"

"Channeling the negotiator."

"Huh?"

"Will explain later."

"You'd better. Those words sound mysterious."

"I'm handling part two of the mystery now, so when we meet I can share the whole story. Busy later?"

"Not really. Just text me where and I'll head over."

"Perfect."

Quinn walked into Drake Realty with authority and confidence, having reminded herself that when it came to arguments, she won most of them.

"Good afternoon," she said pleasantly to the receptionist seated in the lobby area. "I'm here to see Ike Drake."

"Senior or Junior?"

"Junior," Quinn answered, sure the virile man she encountered couldn't have a grown son.

"Do you have an appointment?"

"No." The receptionist reached for the phone. "But I'd rather you not announce me. My visit won't take long."

"I'm sorry, but all visitors must be announced and cleared before they're allowed past this lobby. One moment."

"Then consider me a friend, or family member, I really don't care. Just point me in the direction of Ike Drake's office, now."

"Ma'am, I'm so sorry, but…"

Quinn's anger, which had begun to cool on the drive over, started simmering once again. If announced, she doubted Ike would agree to see her. Anyone who had the nerve to follow up a gift of flowers with a lawsuit was definitely not the kind of man who'd want to face her head-on. "Never mind. It's obvious your job is to protect scoundrels. Some people will do anything for a paycheck. I'll catch him later."

Just as Quinn turned to go, one of two doors on either side of the receptionist's desk opened. Ike.

Their eyes met. The room temperature seemed to rise by several degrees. Quinn was surprised to feel her heartbeat increase. Anger had never felt quite like this.

The receptionist glanced between the two, not sure of what was happening or, given the look that was being exchanged, what might occur. "Mr. Drake, would you like me to—"

"No," he replied, with a hand out to silence the receptionist. He walked over and stood in front of Quinn. "I'm fine. Ms. Taylor, I assume you're here to see me."

Quinn walked forward until their faces were mere inches apart, her voice a whisper beneath her smile. "You know damned well why I'm here." She fixed him with a look that melted most men.

Ike was ice. He gave a curt nod. "Let's talk in my office." Then to the receptionist, "Hold my calls."

He reached the door and held it open for Quinn to enter. She did so, and even though highly frustrated admired the revered mahogany walls and marble-trimmed halls of the prestigious firm. Aware of the curious stares from the employees who passed them, she kept her eyes firmly on Ike's back. Had they been daggers, he would have been punctured from back to front.

He'd barely looked at her. Acted like she was invisible. Quinn wasn't used to being dismissed.

With a discipline honed through years of ballet training and mastering the violin, she kept her ire in check until he'd closed his office door. Then she threw charm school right out the window and exploded like a clobbered piñata at a child's birthday party.

"How dare you sue me over a traffic accident."

"If what took place was a mere traffic incident, you wouldn't be here."

"Look, we don't have to do this. I'll fix your car, no problem. If you're worried that I won't, draw up a contract or something for me to sign. We can't take this to trial. They'll suspend my license. I have too much to do. Let's just drop it. Okay?"

Ike walked behind his desk, sat and began placing items into a briefcase. "It's not up to me. If it was, I'd probably give you a higher fine and harsher sentence than the judge will apply."

"You know what? You're disgusting."

Ike sat back. "I'm disgusting?"

"Absolutely. That you would have the nerve to take me to court for an accident, then sue me on top of it, makes you not only disgusting but a first-class jerk."

Ike was too incredulous to be angry and too stunned to take offense, not only at Ms. Taylor's ability to stand in his office as though she was a victim but that she could do so and look absolutely magnificent.

Time to get out of here. Being alone with this woman behind closed doors was a bad idea. He stood and walked over to take his suit coat off the rack.

"For the record," he began, putting it on, "I couldn't care less what you think of me, but you will respect this business. You had no right coming here to discuss a personal matter, and the boorish manner in which you spoke with the receptionist was out of line. You may have experienced success with it other places, but that bratty behavior doesn't work here." He picked up his briefcase, keys and sunglasses. After a quick look around the office, he headed toward the door. "I suggest any rebuttal you have be shared with your attorney to present at pretrial. Because this conversation is over. I'll walk you out."

Quinn straightened to her full five feet seven inches, plus four-inch heels, and looked Ike directly in the eye. "Bratty, huh? Maybe I am. But you're the one who spent half a million bucks on a relic and threw a weeklong tantrum over a car that's insured, over repairs that will cost you nothing. There are not many people driving cars with a price tag that equals the GNP of third-world nations. I might be spoiled." She placed a finger on his chest. "But one could say the same about you."

Ike took a step back. Not because he was in any way intimidated. Her crystal-covered bravado reminded him of London, his kid sister, who was also headstrong even when wrong. But her temper didn't move him, either.

The reason he'd retreated from the news item in front of him, one he was sure had caused more than one controversial headline, was because of a breaking story he hadn't expected—a magnetic attraction combined with a visceral connection he did not understand. It was a feeling that puzzled him, and if he were honest, frightened him, too. Ike Drake Jr. moved through life with deliberate, thoughtful and strategic precision. He was a grown man, not a teenage boy given to uncontrollable urges. So why did he want nothing more than to wrap his arms around this bundle of fiery femininity and shut her mouth by covering it with his own? Annihilate her anger with his tongue? He felt an inexplicable desire in every inch of his six-foot-plus frame. Several inches in a certain area more than others.

He took a deep breath and released it slowly. His gaze unwavering. His expression unreadable. His eyes slid to her succulent lips. The bottom one trembled. He wasn't the only one affected. She wasn't the only one who mattered. This was a fact she needed to know.

He took a step toward her, so close that their noses almost touched. This time it was Quinn who retreated. He took another step.

"What are you doing?" she asked, the merest hint of uncertainty in her eyes.

Ike said nothing. His expression remained somber, his body taut, exuding power and raw masculinity. He watched as in mere seconds a myriad of emotions flared in her eyes. Suddenly she whirled around, heading for the door. A firm grasp on her arm stayed her progress. It wasn't a move Ike had intended. It just happened. As if his arm didn't want her out of its reach. Later, this would cause Ike concern. Every decision he made was measured and calculated, every move controlled. Yet five minutes alone with this woman had tested his restraint. Had made him react in the heat of the moment. Ike was hot not only under the collar, but in places farther down.

"Let go of my arm!"

"Not until I make myself clear. You are never again to come into this company unannounced and demand anything. If you have something to discuss, schedule an appointment. Unless it is regarding the accident. In that case, don't bother. That matter will be settled in court. Do you understand?"

He felt her body shaking. Judging from the hardened nipples now pressed against her shirt, this wasn't a reaction to what he'd said. It was because of a synergy—stimulating, powerful, undeniable—existing between them. He felt it, too. She leaned forward, her lips so close he felt her breath. His groin stirred. Her mouth opened.

"Let. Me. Go."

Their eyes locked. The room faded away. Time stopped, too. She blinked. He followed the movement of her long lashes. The urge to know if her lips tasted as sweet as they looked was overwhelming. Time to make a move.

Two quick taps on the door and it swung open. "Hey, Ike…whoa!" The tableau before him stopped Terrell in his tracks. "Sorry, brother. I didn't know—"

"Your timing is perfect," Ike interrupted, wanting to hug his brother and throttle him, too. The sound of the door opening had snapped Ike out of the Quinn-induced haze that had him about to act totally out of character. Regaining his composure, he walked behind his desk and began shuffling papers. "Ms. Taylor was just on her way out."

Terrell turned to her with hand outstretched. "Hello, Ms. Taylor. I'm Terrell Drake."

"I'm out of here." She brushed past him and out of Ike's office.

Terrell's expression was one of amusement as he watched her leave. Still smiling, he turned back to his brother.

"Don't." Ike reached for his charging cell phone that he'd almost forgotten.

"What, bro?" Terrell innocently replied. "I didn't even say anything."

Ike pocketed the phone, placed the charger in his briefcase and snapped it shut. "Let's keep it that way. Unless it's about the deal."

No doubt the upcoming meeting was important. The Drakes had handled their share of large purchases, but the office building strategically situated in San Francisco's business district would be one of their biggest ones yet.

"That's why I came by, to make sure there were no loose ends regarding the presentation."

Ike gave him a look. "You know better than that."

"I thought so. Until I walked in as you were about to get your groove on in the middle of the day." Ike walked by him and toward the door. Terrell fell into step behind him. "Wait. Ms. Taylor as in Quinn Taylor, the girl who hit you?"

"Focus, Terrell. Your mind should be on numbers and tenant projections. Not her."

"Oh, like yours was a minute ago?"

Ike ignored Terrell as they reached their father's corner office. Ike Drake Sr. was just coming out of his private restroom, looking the part of a dynasty head in a navy blue suit, tailored to obscure his expanding stomach, stark white shirt and a red-white-and-blue tie. His salt-and-pepper hair was cut and lined, his face clean-shaven save for a thin mustache. At not quite six feet, it wasn't his stature that made his presence so commanding, but the steely confidence that oozed from his pores. It's what made him such a stellar negotiator and businessman, and why they were on their way to sealing one of their most lucrative deals yet.

"About time you two got here," he barked gruffly.

"Sorry about that, Dad," Ike Jr. offered. "Had to handle some unexpected business."

"He was handling it, all right," Terrell murmured, halted from commenting further by his brother's warning stare.

"I understand, son," Ike Sr. drawled as he reached for his personal items on the desk and walked toward them. "The meeting we're heading to involves a negotiation for only a hundred million or so. No big deal."

Ike Sr.'s offhand comment lightened the mood. The men chatted casually as a town car transported them to the private airstrip where they boarded a company plane for San Francisco. Once aboard, Ike Sr. and Terrell pulled out their computers. Ike stared out the window, his mind on Quinn and what happened at the office. She was a study in contrasts. Exasperating yet intriguing. Bothersome but beguiling. With a slight shake of his head, he forced himself back into the present. Earlier he'd told Terrell to focus. Right now he needed to follow that same advice.

Chapter 5

Quinn entered the cool confines of Acquired Taste, one of only a handful of restaurants in the town of Paradise Cove, now boasting close to five thousand residents. It was lunchtime. The room was crowded. Peyton had arrived earlier to secure a table. Quinn spotted her and headed over.

"Hey." Quinn plopped into the empty booth seat.

Peyton stopped texting and looked up. "Whoa. Somebody's not happy." She set her phone on the table. "Looks like the negotiation didn't go so well."

"Not at all."

"What happened?"

"I was involved in an accident. Of all the cars in this town, I had to hit an antique owned by an asshole. The guy's impossible."

"More impossible than you?" Quinn cut her eyes at Peyton. "Don't act like that's an exaggeration. I love hanging around you. But for the average person...you're hard-core."

"I'll take that as a compliment."

"You're welcome." They paused and ordered drinks from the waitress. "Who was the lucky guy you met by accident?" Air quotes emphasized the last two words. "Pun intended."

Quinn gave her a look. Peyton laughed. Quinn obviously saw nothing funny. Peyton lost her smile. "I'm sorry. Bad timing."

"Bad joke, too."

"Whose car did you hit?"

"Whose car did I collide with while swerving to save an

animal's life? Ike Drake. He's also the man who's decided to personally sue me because of it."

"That's crazy."

"It's to ensure that his car gets fixed."

Peyton made a face. "Um, that's why we have insurance."

"Like I said, his is some kind of rare antique. Repairs will be expensive."

Peyton shrugged. "You've got the cash."

"I'm not worried about that. But they're threatening to take my driver's license. Trent's coming to visit next week. That won't work at all."

Peyton reached for the menu and began to scan it. "You mean I finally get to meet your bestie? Cool!"

"Not so cool with what's going on."

"You'll get out of it. You always do."

Quinn picked up hers, as well. "I hope you're right."

"It could be worse. Ike Drake is handsome and one of this town's most eligible bachelors."

"His personality isn't nearly as attractive."

"I wouldn't mind being with someone like him."

"If the opportunity arises in the middle of my trial, I'll be sure and pass that along. Through his prosecuting attorney, of course."

"I'm just kidding, silly."

"Don't mind me. Go ahead and sleep with the enemy. And from what I've seen of his stodgy personality, I mean that literally."

No sooner had the words come out of her mouth than an image of Ike's face popped into her mind. The one he'd worn earlier when clearly chagrined that she'd stopped by his workplace. Fiery dark eyes. The hint of a cleft in his jutted chin. Well-defined lips. And words delivered in a way that brooked no argument, from a man clearly used to being in control. In Quinn's first serious relationship, she'd worn the pants. Her ex-fiancé had let her do what she wanted. Quinn liked calling the shots—after a childhood in which she had no voice, she liked control. Remembering the power in Ike's strong body and the force of his stern words made Quinn realize she might enjoy a man who took control.

"You okay?"

Quinn looked up to see the waiter by their table. "I'm fine," she answered Peyton. "Just had a crazy thought, that's all. You go first."

Peyton looked amused. "I've already ordered."

"Oh." Quinn took another quick look at the menu. "I'll have the baked salmon."

"With a side of Ike?" Peyton asked.

"You're nuts."

"Maybe. But the look on your face just now got me thinking that you and Ike might be more alike than you know."

"I couldn't care less. By this time next week, that'll be behind me."

She delivered this statement with complete confidence and secretly hoped the fire in her belly from the encounter with Ike would leave just as quickly.

Later that afternoon in San Francisco, the Drake men were in a festive mood. The meetings had gone better than expected. Before heading back to PC, the men had decided to have dinner at one of Ike Sr.'s favorite restaurants. "The best Italian food outside of Italy" was how he described it. The Ikes and Terrell watched the sommelier uncork a vintage cabernet sauvignon blend. A single bottle cost more than some paid for rent, but next to a wine their Southern California cousins produced, it was Ike Sr.'s favorite. The complex, rich flavor was achieved through extensive knowledge, deft blending and patience. Ike thought the pairing a perfect choice.

He held up his glass. "To our new silent partner, Global 100, their rep, Bernard Lindsay, and the procurement of Ten Drake Plaza. The financing has been solidified. We'll be able to close in less than sixty days. Good work, sons."

Terrell held up his glass.

Ike held back. “You said it yourself, Dad. We’ve got sixty days or less until it’s official. Let’s toast then.”

“Ah, man!” Terrell shook his head as he and his dad clinked glasses. “Stop being so pessimistic, bro. Getting to this point took three years. Let’s celebrate.”

“It’s not pessimism, it’s pragmatism. I don’t like counting chickens before they’re hatched.”

“Ike tends to be more cautious,” Ike Sr. said. “On the other hand, you, Terrell, are more instinctive. You sometimes act first and think later. Both qualities have advantages and disadvantages. That’s why we make such a great team.”

“What quality do you bring to the table, Dad?” Terrell asked.

Ike Sr. answered without a pause. “My checkbook.”

They laughingly toasted to this truth.

Ike swirled the wine and took another taste. “This is very nice, Dad.”

Ike Sr. looked over the rim of the glasses he’d donned to read the menu. “Glad you approve.”

“It’s all right,” Terrell said. “Though it doesn’t beat a good shot of Louis XIII.”

“I’ll admit that cognac pairs well with a Cuban cigar, but for the perfectly cooked trio of duck, lobster and venison that I’m about to enjoy, this—” he raised the glass in Terrell’s direction before taking a sip “—is the perfect choice.”

“How’d you find out about this place?” Terrell asked, casually taking in the room.

“Came to a meeting here several years ago.”

Terrell nodded. “A business meeting?”

“A discussion about networking that could have led to business deals, but more about how we could impact the young men in this area, especially Oakland.”

Ike looked up from his cell phone. “I don’t remember you ever working with men from here.”

"You were busy in the field then, son. Working hard to come up in the company and make a name for yourself. It was right around the time you negotiated the deal on our office building."

"Then it's no wonder. Until it closed and we had the keys, that deal was the only thing on my mind."

"Not much has changed," Terrell teased.

Ike ignored him. "Are you still in contact with any of them? Perhaps those affiliations can be of future benefit. As our Bay Area portfolio grows, our presence will as well."

"Quite possibly," his father replied with a nod. "One of them has become especially successful in the ten years or so since that meeting. Though I'm glad not to have needed him. He's a high-powered criminal defense attorney, mostly white collar. Became a judge a few years ago."

"Who?"

"You've met him a time or two," Ike Sr. answered. "Glen Taylor."

Ike sat back, deflated. "Her father?"

"I think she put a spell on you, brother. Even out of town, you can't get away from Quinn Taylor." Terrell smiled broadly as he emphasized the last name and watched Ike squirm.

Ike Sr. looked between his sons. "What am I missing?"

"Terrell's trying to be funny and not doing a good job. Quinn is the woman who hit the Ferrari and destroyed over a year's worth of restorative work, causing about a hundred thousand dollars' worth of damage in an instant. According to Audrey, she's Glen's daughter. She attended the ball, Dad. You were away from the table when Mrs. Newman introduced her to the family."

"He'd just gotten married when I met him. Don't remember hearing about a daughter, though our interaction has been limited. A couple golf tournaments, some charity events."

"He's hoping they're not related," Terrell explained. "Ike sued Quinn to make sure he gets paid."

"I'm protecting my investment."

"That's a wise move, son. The value of rare cars like that only increases, especially those in pristine condition." The elder Drake studied the label on the bottle of wine. "It will be a bit awkward, however, if that is his daughter."

"Trust me, Dad. There's no way. She's wild, impetuous, unreasonable..."

Ike Sr. gave his son a level stare. "Have you forgotten that your mother and I raised London?"

"You tried," Terrell responded, "but our dear sister is in a whole other category. I'm still not convinced that someone didn't drop her off on our doorstep after spending those early formative years being raised by wolves."

London was the youngest Drake sibling, ten years Ike's junior and a bundle of drama from the time she was born. At thirteen, her front-page antics and headstrong defiance to parental rules had her shipped off to a prestigious boarding school. What was supposed to be a form of punishment designed to tame their wild child had the opposite effect. Just before graduating high school, she was discovered by a modeling scout and given a contract. Mere days after "Pomp and Circumstance," she landed in Milan, dived headfirst into the party scene and continued to make headlines. During her last visit it appeared that she'd calmed down a bit. But not much.

The first course of their prix fixe meal arrived, shifting conversation from wayward women to exquisite appetizers such as beets with smoked parsnip and cocoa crumb, beef tartare with chickpeas and black olives, and smoked pork belly on a radicchio-and-pickled-apple bed. By the time desserts arrived, Terrell and Ike Sr. had all but convinced Ike Jr. that closing the Ten Drake Plaza deal was a fait accompli.

At the same time, Ike had convinced himself that love for his Ferrari was what kept Quinn on his mind. He'd also bought into the convenient illusion that Quinn and Judge Taylor were not related. Were that the case, he'd drop the suit and work out an amicable arrangement to have his car repaired. But Ike felt sure that the chances of Quinn being Glen's daughter were none and none. There was no turning back. Quinn Taylor needed to learn a lesson. They would go to trial.

Chapter 6

Two weeks later, Ike pulled into the parking lot of the town's municipal building ready to put the accident behind him. He'd been so immersed in the details of securing the funding from Global 100 and closing the San Francisco deal that today's meeting had barely crossed his mind.

But Quinn had. More than he cared to admit. All the more reason to get this done. The town was small and the Drakes knew her grandmother, Maggie Newman, but Ike couldn't imagine he and Quinn ran in the same circles. Except in passing, it was very unlikely he'd see her again. That she'd agreed to plead no contest and to the pretrial was a relief. He imagined the proceedings would be brief, repayment for the car damage and some type of probation or community service.

He entered the lobby, waved at a couple people he knew and continued across the room and down a hall to where Matthew's assistant sat at her desk.

"Hello, Mr. Drake. Go right in. Mr. Holden has already arrived."

"What about the defendant and her attorney?"

"Not yet, but they're on their way."

Ike gave a nod and opened the door to the chambers of Matthew White, the judge who'd be hearing the case. He wasn't there. Lance was, and on his cell phone. He waved a greeting, held up a finger and continued the call. Ike sat, pulled out his phone and began to check the emails he'd ignored all morning.

Lance ended the call. "Sorry about that, Ike. I'm in the

rare position of having back-to-back meetings just about all day long."

"Business is booming, huh?"

"You might say that. Not as exciting as your life, I'm sure."

"My life is full, but whether or not it's exciting depends on one's definition of the word."

"Hey, you were this year's grand marshal. That's heady stuff!"

Ike chuckled. "It was an honor, but let's face it. Paradise Cove isn't San Francisco or LA."

Lance began to respond but stopped when the door opened. Both men turned as attorney Joey Wang stepped back from the door to allow Quinn to enter. Ike inwardly applauded his outer expression and the ability to look passive as his insides churned. Skirt too short. Legs too long. Top too tight. Shiny stilettos that could double as stilts. In a word? She looked inappropriately dressed and amazing. Ike felt Lance rise beside him. He stood, too.

"Ms. Taylor," he said formally as they shook hands.

"Mr. Drake," she responded, all sugar and spice. Except for her casual attire, she was the epitome of professionalism, a total opposite of the tornado who'd whirled into his office demanding he drop all charges and pull his lawsuit.

"A positive beginning," Joey said while looking bemused. "Let's hope this civility continues throughout the proceedings."

"Civil is my middle name, Joey," Ike responded. He looked at Quinn and continued, "I'll do my part."

The look she returned was unreadable, but there were millions to be made if he could bottle that smile.

A side door opened. The judge entered. That he wasn't wearing the standard black robe indicated informality. The look on his face underscored the point that informal did not mean unimportant. He walked directly to the black leather chair behind the imposing oak desk between two flags and sat down.

After taking a moment to review copies of the motions that had been placed on the desk, he began.

"Good afternoon, Attorney Wang, Attorney Holden." They responded. "Mr. Drake."

"Judge White."

His voice softened. "Ms. Taylor."

"Afternoon, Judge," was her softly spoken reply.

"We're here on the matter involving Ike Drake Jr. and Kristin Quinn Taylor. I have reviewed the motions set forth, and if there are no further motions or addendums thereto, am ready to render a judgment." He looked at the attorneys.

"None here, Judge," Lance said.

Joey shook his head.

After reading another page of legal jargon regarding Quinn's no-contest plea, Matthew gave his decision.

"As a result of the accident and the damage sustained to Mr. Drake's vehicle, the defendant is ordered to make full restitution regarding all repairs and/or replacement as set forth in the motion by Mr. Holden and agreed to by Mr. Wang and his client. Furthermore, I believe excessive speed played a part in this accident. Ms. Taylor testified to the presence of a dog running into the street, which caused her to swerve and her vehicle to cross into the oncoming lane. The investigation yielded no proof as to the existence of said dog."

"He thinks I'm lying?" Quinn blurted to her attorney. And then to the judge, "There was a dog!"

"Quinn," her attorney warned.

"Ms. Taylor," the judge called simultaneously. "Please refrain from further outbursts. As to your question to Attorney Wang, my statement is based not on whether or not you are lying, but whether or not evidence of the dog in question was uncovered. It was not."

Quinn huffed and crossed her arms but remained quiet.

"Thankfully no one was seriously injured, which makes this case simpler, in that what happened calls for no jail time or probation. However, due to the defendant's previous history of driving at excessive speeds, and the traffic violations that occurred as a result, I am going to impose a penalty in addition to the monetary obligations."

Quinn's indignant gasp cut through the judge's droning voice. From the corner of his eye, Ike saw Joey place a hand on her arm. To calm or warn? Probably both. Quinn turned and caught the smirk on his face. She glared. Ike's Cheshire grin widened into a satisfied smile. He sat back and watched Quinn try to control her mounting anger. What would be her punishment? Garbage detail? Flipping burgers? Emptying bedpans as a hospital aide? The thought of her being subjugated to most people's normal almost made Ike laugh out loud. His day had been stressful. Now he felt relief.

Judge White continued.

"Usually, this type of consequence involves some form of community service—ground clearance, graffiti removal, recycling projects and the like. But it is my belief that despite the defendant's propensity for having what my father calls a lead foot, Ms. Taylor is an intelligent individual with analytical and persuasive skills that could be put to better use in a complementary setting. Therefore, I am ordering Ms. Taylor to complete a four-week work assignment, each week consisting of forty hours, beginning Monday of next week.

"Furthermore, while not suspended, Ms. Taylor's driving license will be on restricted status for thirty days, during which driving is permitted to and from work only."

Lance raised a finger. "Judge, do you have an employer lined up and will this work be monitored? How can my client be assured that this penalty is carried out and completed?"

"Good question, Lance. That's a problem I've easily solved by choosing Drake Realty Plus as the business for this detail."

Ike sat up slowly. His body rigid. His mind disbelieving.

It was Quinn's turn to smirk.

"I don't understand," Joey said.

"Neither do I," Ike intoned.

"You will supervise the work detail, Mr. Drake," Matthew continued. "What better way to make sure that the plaintiff's call for justice has been satisfied than to appoint him as the defendant's supervisor?"

"Wait a minute, Judge," Ike said, tossing out all formality, barely maintaining respect. "That can't happen. It makes no sense at all."

"It can't, and it won't," Quinn added, with a glance toward Ike, who now spoke quietly yet fervently in Lance's ear.

"Quinn, quiet," Joey admonished.

"I won't work for him," she hissed.

Matthew proved that he'd heard her by his swift, stern response. "You'll do that or go to jail, young lady."

This comment brought Joey to his feet. "Your Honor, if I may approach the, um, the desk."

Matthew gathered strewn papers into a stack and tidied his desk. "Mr. Wang, that won't be necessary."

The statement made Ike's attorney pop up faster than bread in a toaster. "Your Honor, this is a thoughtful approach to rectifying an unfortunate situation. My client appreciates your diligence to justice being served. However, we regretfully cannot accept this solution. Mr. Drake is under intense pressure right now to meet a deadline for a major project with millions of dollars at stake. This is absolutely the worst time for him to be distracted with an additional responsibility. If it pleases the court, we'd like to offer an alternative location, Drake Ranch. This business includes a vineyard, stables and adequate work opportunities through which Ms. Taylor can fulfill the penalty you've imposed."

"Thank you, Mr. Holden. However, this matter has already been discussed with Ike Drake Sr., who has approved the arrangement. He has the utmost confidence, as do I, that both parties will handle themselves in a manner that will prove beneficial to all." He placed the papers he'd gathered into a folder, looked at his watch and stood. "Now, everyone, if you'll excuse me, I'm running late for a meeting with some council members. My assistant will provide all relevant copies of the order that has been put forth."

Before Ike, Quinn or either of the attorneys could wrap their heads around what had just happened, the judge was gone.

Chapter 7

"He's in his study, honey."

Ike strode past Jennifer without a proper hello. He was sure the look on his face had prompted his mother to point him in the direction of the answers he sought. The pretrial meeting had ended three hours ago. That business had precluded him from getting answers until now had only caused his anger and frustration to reach the boiling point.

He didn't bother to knock. "Dad, what were you thinking?"

"Now hold on, son," Ike Sr. said as he threw up a hand to ward off the verbal attack. "I know why you're here. I know why you're upset. Have a seat."

"I really don't feel like sitting, Dad."

Ike Sr. gave his son a look as he stood and headed to an ornate cherrywood butler table bearing a crystal decanter set that had belonged to his wife's great-grandmother. "I didn't ask whether or not you felt like it."

Ike plopped into a leather chair and sulked.

"Want a spot of brandy?"

"No, thanks."

Ike stretched out his legs and forced himself to calm down. There was no hurrying Ike Drake Sr., and staying wound up wasn't good for his health. He pulled out his cell phone and texted Warren. After leaving his parents' home, he'd release the day's tension by going to Warren's ranch and helping to break in his newly purchased home gym.

Ike Sr. returned to his seat. He took a sip of his drink and then set the snifter on the table beside him. He turned his body toward Ike and said, "Quinn Taylor is Glen Taylor's daughter."

Ike silently absorbed this news, thinking that in turning down the liquor he might have spoken too soon. "So what Audrey said was true."

"Yes. I spoke to Glen."

"You talked to her father?"

"I did. Apparently he'd contacted the court and discussed her case with the judge, and I guess together they concocted this rather unusual arrangement."

"I don't get it. Why would he want his daughter to work for us?"

"Some of what he shared was in confidence, but suffice it to say that he believes Quinn could benefit from being in a professional environment, one that requires discipline and focus. He admits she has faults but says hers was not always the easiest life."

Ike's look conveyed he didn't believe that for a minute. "She's lived in the lap of luxury."

"Money isn't everything, son."

"True. Where's her mom?"

Ike Sr. opened a humidor and pulled out a cigar. "I didn't ask and he didn't offer. He did share that his daughter is very smart and highly educated."

"Audrey mentioned she'd returned to the States to get her degree."

Ike Sr. nodded.

"Dad, I can understand that given she's Glen's daughter you'd want to help, but have you forgotten what's at stake in the upcoming weeks?"

"Of course not. I would not have agreed to Glen's request were I not absolutely sure that his daughter was capable of assisting us in the endeavor.

"Oh, and there's one more thing. She isn't to know of her dad's involvement. Again, he didn't explain and I didn't pry, but I get the feeling that theirs is not the best of relationships. But it is clear that he loves his child."

Ike rubbed his forehead, absorbing what his dad had shared. "I can't believe this."

Ike Sr. clipped a cigar. He lit it and exhaled slowly. "Whenever you start to get frustrated about this situation, remember that it was your idea."

"How do you figure?"

"You wanted her to receive some type of punishment, right? Felt that she'd probably not experienced enough consequences for her actions? That's what the judge told Glen."

"Yeah, I said it," Ike replied. "I just had no idea at the time that her punishment would also be mine."

Quinn angrily swiped clothes-filled hangers from one side of the rack to the other. It had been three days since the circus of a pretrial conference in Judge White's office, when he'd handed down the ridiculous sentence of working for Ike Drake. When she said she'd rather go to jail, she meant it. She'd even relented in being angry at her father long enough to call him and try to enlist his aid. It was her mess, he'd told her, and he wouldn't help clean it up. Time for her to learn responsibility, he'd added. How did he think she'd earned her bachelor's and master's degrees in just six years? By being a scatterbrain?

"Quinn, dear, are you here?"

"In the closet!"

Seconds later Maggie stepped inside a closet larger than some bedrooms. "I thought I heard someone in here. Aren't you supposed to be at the airport, picking up your best friend?"

"Trent? No. His uncle asked for help with a business project somewhere on the East Coast. It was just as well, since for the next thirty days I'll be on lockdown with a fire-breathing dragon named Drake. Hopefully he'll be back this way by then. He can't wait to meet you." Quinn pulled a dress off its hanger, placed it against her body and looked in the mirror. "Ugh! I have nothing to wear!"

Maggie chuckled as she looked around. "Dear, you have enough here to open a consignment store."

"I meant anything to wear while giving the Drakes four weeks of free labor."

"Oh, Quinn. Surely you're not still smarting over what happened in court. It could have been much worse. Imagine someone without your resources. They'd be facing a mountain of debt and possible jail time."

"One moment I'm fine, and then I think about the circumstances and get angry all over again. That I'm doing anything more than repairing the car I hit and maybe paying a fine is ridiculous. And there *was* a dog." She reached for another dress, checked herself in the mirror and tossed it on a growing pile. "And then there's Dad's reaction. Refusing to get involved. It's like there's a conspiracy to make me miserable."

"Ha! That's a stretch, Quinn." Maggie sat on a vanity chair.

"Okay, maybe a little. But it's still not fair."

"Life isn't always fair, honey. But a lesson I've learned that has served me well is that it isn't what happens to us but how we react. In this instance, you can either pout and fuss and spend the next four weeks being miserable in your quest to be right. Or you can take this lemon, make lemonade and serve it to all of the doubters while dressed to the nines and wearing a smile."

Maggie rose, walked to the far end of the rack and pulled out a knee-length dress with cap sleeves. A sheath design, the stretch-woven material was a rich shade of indigo blue. "How about this one, Kristin Quinn? It's quite appropriate for the office. The color is divine and would bring out the bronze tones in your skin."

Quinn turned to where Maggie stood behind her. "Oh, my goodness! Where'd you find this?" She took the dress

Maggie offered and held it up to her body. "I can't believe I still have this thing!"

"That thing," her grandmother replied in the same derogatory tone Quinn had used, "will look amazing on you."

Quinn walked to the mirror and held up the dress again. "Remember Libby, my roommate during senior year?" Maggie nodded. "Her mother brought this dress for me when Libby and I were invited to attend a royal tea with *madame la maire de Genève*." Using the fluent French honed during her years in Switzerland, Quinn pronounced the mayoral title with dramatic flair as she executed a perfect pirouette. "She called it an investment piece, a classic."

"She's right. The cut, length, color…all timeless. It reminds me…" Maggie placed a hand to her mouth as if to prevent the words from spilling out of their own accord.

"What, Grandmother?"

"You don't like to speak of it, dear."

Quinn sobered. "Mom?" Maggie nodded. "It's easier when I don't remember."

"If you say so."

"I keep thinking there will come a time when I won't miss her as much and it will be easier to talk about her."

"My dear Kristin Quinn, you will always miss her. It's been almost thirty years since I lost Mama, and still, I miss her every single day. Not with sadness, but with love. With every thought I have, she lives. Each time I imagine her face or speak her name—Lois—she lives."

Thoughts of yesteryear evaporated conversation. Quinn slid to the floor and wrapped her arms around her knees. Several minutes ticked by, both women absorbed in a movie of memories. When Quinn finally broke the silence, her voice was soft, reflective.

"Sometimes I can't remember her face. At other times it comes in clearly, like a photograph. Her long, silky hair that I loved to brush, and the jewelry box on her vanity with the ballerina. My desire to learn ballet began with the first twirl of that miniature doll. She had a ring similar to the color of this dress, in fact."

"Yes, a sapphire. It was her birthstone."

"Round, surrounded by diamonds, I'd put it on my thumb and pretend it was my wedding day. She asked who the groom was. I told her it was Daddy. She laughed and laughed. And so pretty."

"She was a beautiful one, your mother. But also smart, strong, with a delightful sense of humor. Beautiful Brenda, Glen called her, and soon I adopted the name, as well. From the moment my son saw her, he didn't stand a chance. He fell in love with her, and so did I. When you came along, I fell in love all over again."

Quinn dropped her face into her hands. Soft sobs slipped between her fingers. Maggie hurried over and knelt down to comfort her.

"See, I told you it would make me sad!"

"It's all right, dear one. Tears water the soul. And just for a moment, were you not happy? Couldn't you almost feel her here as we remembered?"

Quinn looked up through teary wonder-filled eyes, nodded slowly and whispered, "Almost."

Maggie stood and removed the dress from Quinn's hand. "I think you should wear this tomorrow and think of that ring, and marriage to your father—" both women chuckled "—and all of the other happy times. Paired with a blazer and sensible pumps, you will be ready for corporate America. Everyone will notice that a smart, beautiful and capable woman is in their midst. Tomorrow you can present yourself as a pouting girl or a powerful woman. The choice is up to you."

Quinn stood and hugged Maggie. "Thank you, Grandmother."

Quinn tried on the dress. It still fit perfectly and looked almost new. Following Maggie's advice, she chose a black knit jacket with multicolored thread woven throughout. A pair of classic black pumps and simple silver jewelry completed the look.

Once done, she took a shower. Her thoughts meandered from her grandmother, to her mother, to the dress that opened up a touchy topic—the man behind the reason the dress was picked out. She was still peeved about having driving restrictions and a forced internship for the next thirty days, a situation for which she blamed Ike Drake. In hindsight, she felt she could have brought a stronger argument than her attorney did. If she could have found that blasted dog, she might even have won. But there was more than one way to make one's point, and it was never too late for victory. Ike Drake didn't know it, but in filing suit and suggesting penalties, he'd thrown down the gauntlet. Quinn decided to pick it up. Tomorrow, it would be game on.

Chapter 8

Mondays had never been Ike's favorite day of the week. Today held even less appeal. Along with what he knew would be a grueling morning meeting, one in which the details of closing the Ten Drake Plaza purchase would be laid out, and where the responsibilities of who'd handle what would be delegated, there was the irksome matter of having to put up with that Taylor woman for the next four weeks.

The timing couldn't have been worse. There were a myriad of details for any real estate transaction, but when it involved one of the tallest office buildings in a popular city's coveted financial district and over a hundred million dollars, it required almost as much manpower and time as all their other deals combined. He couldn't afford to lose focus for even a second and felt he'd come up with a solution that would benefit everyone, but mostly himself.

He entered the company through a private side door and walked to his assistant's desk. "Good morning, Lydia."

"Hey, Ike. You're looking sharp. I thought the meeting was here today."

"It is."

"Oh."

Ike smiled. "Knowing how rarely I wear a suit, I guess I deserve that reaction."

"I'm sorry. I didn't mean anything by it. You look really nice. That look is more Terrell or Niko's style, that's all. You've always been more of a preppy dresser, a casual-pant-and-polo type of guy."

"You've been with me in the trenches for five years now. So you should know."

"Well, if it means anything, I think you should dress up more often. You look like the chief operating officer of a very successful real estate company."

"I am the COO of a real estate company."

She smiled triumphantly. "I rest my case."

"Good, because we've got a busy day ahead." He looked at his watch. "Do you have the files I requested over the weekend?"

She reached for a pile of folders stacked neatly in a tray on her desk and held them out to him. "Here you go."

"Thanks. I'll be in my office for the next hour. Hold my calls. Remember we've got Ms. Taylor coming in, the one from the accident."

"I still don't understand what Matt was smoking when he handed down that decision. Who does community service in a corporate office?"

Lydia, five years older than Ike, had also grown up in Paradise Cove and had known the White family since childhood. As often happened in small towns, there was usually only one or two degrees of separation between residents. In Lydia's case, she'd had a crush on Matthew's older brother. They'd casually dated during her junior year of high school.

"It's what it is, so we'll deal with it. As busy as we've been all year, I'm sure you can find enough to keep her busy, tucked away in a file room or similar place where she won't be able to cause trouble."

Lydia frowned. "What kind of trouble could she possibly cause?"

Just then, Ike's line beeped. Lydia answered it. "Ike Drake's office, Lydia speaking." She listened and stood. "Okay, I'll be right up.

"Looks like I'm about to get my answer. Our potential troublemaker is up front."

* * *

"Feel free to have a seat if you'd like. Someone will be up for you shortly."

"Thank you."

Quinn smiled at the cheerful receptionist, then walked toward one of two plush chenille-covered chairs. Amid the stainless steel, dark wood and gray walls, the deep rose color of the cushions was unexpected. She looked to the wall behind her and noted how that same color was highlighted in a collage of portraits depicting a sparse, unincorporated Paradise Cove with a lone building on what was now a bustling main street. The subtle yet clear coordination of every item in the foyer and lobby areas made it clear that a professional who knew their stuff had designed a professional, welcoming and sophisticated environment.

"Ms. Taylor? Quinn?"

Quinn looked away from the picture collage to greet an attractive woman, casually dressed, with a smile much more inviting than the tight bun she wore. "Yes, that's me."

"Wow. You're very pretty. That's a gorgeous color."

"Thank you," Quinn said while wondering about the twinkle in the assistant's eye.

"What would you call that shade of blue—royal, maybe?"

The merest of smiles appeared just for a second. "I'd call it sapphire," she said.

"Too fancy for my blood. But you look terrific." She extended a hand. "I'm Lydia, Mr. Drake's executive assistant. He has meetings this morning and asked that I get you started. He'll be back for lunch. You two will meet then. Come on, let's get you set up."

Lydia led them through a door and down a long hall with offices on each side. She kept up a steady chatter as they walked. "Those are cute shoes, too. Don't see how you walk in them, though. You're the total package, that's for sure. From the looks of things, you'll be in the file room mostly—gathering documents, making copies, filing—the exciting stuff. Our dress policy is business casual." She swept a hand over a basic navy pantsuit to make her point. "You can wear suits if you want, but it's not mandatory."

They reached a room at the end of the hall. Lydia opened the door and turned on the light. Unlike the rich, refined colors of the lobby furnishings, the file room was basic squared—cream-colored walls, one lined with what appeared to be a customized file unit. She guessed there were at least thirty individual drawers. Each was marked with a series of letters—an alphabetical system, she assumed. Opposite that wall were three run-of-the-mill desks, flat top, middle drawer, filing drawer on the right. The back wall held another table containing, Quinn assumed, everything one needed to keep information organized. Amid a pile of flattened boxes and stacked trays that held various items she glimpsed staplers, hole punchers, tape dispensers, calculators and at the end a keyboard in front of a forty-inch screen. The worst thing about the room wasn't its color, drabness or the organized chaos on the back table. There were no windows. For this California native and sun child through and through, the next four weeks would feel like jail for real.

She followed Lydia to the desk farthest away from the door. "Let's put you here for now," she said, pointing to the desk. "Feel free to use the drawers for your personal items."

Quinn placed her purse in the empty drawer as Lydia continued.

"Everything in here is pretty straightforward. Folders are filed by company, alphabet and date with the most recent documents at the front. We'll break you into that later, but first off I have a major copying project. I don't know how much Ike has told you about what's going on…"

"I don't know anything. We haven't talked."

"You're interning as some type of community service, correct?"

Quinn resisted the urge to roll her eyes. "Something like that."

"Well, anyway, we are in the last leg of a major real estate purchase, one of the largest that our company has procured. I can't stress how important whatever you get to work on is, or how crucial it is that you pay attention to the smallest detail and make sure items are copied in the correct order, refiled properly, et cetera, okay?" Quinn nodded. "I'll still double-check everything to make sure, but knowing what's at stake will hopefully cause you to take your time and be thorough. Even though these tasks are considered menial—" Lydia used air quotes "—they are all important. Do you have a secretarial or admin background?"

"Nope, this will be my first time filing anything except my nails."

Lydia laughed. "So what are you, a college student, business major, maybe?"

"I've graduated."

"Oh. What's your degree in?"

"Business."

"Oh," Lydia repeated with renewed understanding. "That's why they have you here. Well, great! Hopefully we'll be able to put some of that fresh education to good use."

Lydia wrapped up the introductory session with what she said was most important: breaks, lunches and the location of the restrooms and break areas. Quinn chose to head to the ladies' room while Lydia brought in the copying project. She returned, looked at the mountain of documents and murmured, "How is this my life?"

Thirty minutes into her copying project, Quinn had removed her jacket. The four-inch heels followed ninety minutes later. After three solid hours of standing, sorting, copying and stapling, she was ready to run through the halls buck naked and screaming like a banshee.

Fortunately, she was rescued before the idea could gain a solid hold.

"How's it going?" Lydia asked, as cheerful now as she'd been earlier.

"Okay, I guess."

"Did you take your break?"

Quinn shook her head. "I forgot."

"You've been here copying all this time?" Lydia walked over to the sizable pile of finished items on the right. "You poor thing! I'm surprised you didn't go stir-crazy in here."

"I was close."

"I bet. At least you got comfortable. Good for you. And do take your breaks, okay? Just a walk to the break room or outside for fresh air really makes a difference."

"I'll keep that in mind."

"The good news is that you'll get fresh air now. I've made reservations for you and Ike over at the club. So grab your things and we'll head up front."

A phone called pulled Lydia away from the lobby. Quinn was thankful for the break. She liked her, and appreciated her genuine friendliness. But the constant chatter, boredom, lack of sleep and residual resentment was too much to handle simultaneously. After a quick trip to the restroom to freshen up, she sat down and sent a text to Trent about a masquerade ball Lydia had mentioned. The restriction on her license would be over by then. It would be fun to attend the party with her crazy friend. She sent a smiley face in response to his quick answer, then began posting on social media. Ike arrived fifteen minutes later. She heard him at the receptionist desk inquiring of her whereabouts.

She walked from behind the partition that looked more like a work of modern art.

"I'm here, Ike."

He turned and gave her a quick once-over, his facial expression one that Quinn couldn't read. Given how her body reacted to seeing him, she hoped her thoughts were hidden, as well.

"Good afternoon, Quinn."

"Hello." There wasn't a shy bone in her body. So why did her face suddenly feel flushed, along with heat rising and pulsations happening? This was the guy who'd sued her, who was more uptight than her father and responsible for her spending the past three hours in a cave. She did not like him like that!

"Are you ready?"

She cleared her throat and responded without looking at him. "Yes."

They crossed over to the elevator. She could feel his eyes on her and continued scrolling on her phone. "Were you waiting long?"

"No."

There it was again—that feeling that he wanted to say more and didn't. And even weirder, her ability to sense him so strongly. Was it a full moon or what?

The elevator ride was a quiet one. They walked to a late-model sedan parked in the first reserved slot. He opened her door. She thanked him and got in, still feeling all girly, like she was out on a date with someone who mattered. Obviously the six months since her broken engagement, during which she'd sworn off men to get her head together, had scrambled her brain. She needed to get out more. Seriously.

They headed out of the parking lot. "Given our contentious beginning, I thought a lunch meeting would be a good way to set a friendlier tone for the next four weeks." She nodded but said nothing. "Do you agree?"

"I think it's a good idea."

"Good. How are you settling in so far?"

"Fine…thanks."

She glimpsed Ike's curious expression from the corner of her eyes. She didn't blame him for being confused. She was asking herself who the woman was riding in his car and where the hell was Quinn?

What was it about Ike Drake that so moved her? As she listened to the quiet, tranquil music coming from the car stereo, the reason hit her like a punch in the gut. In past relationships, she'd been in control. Hotly pursued. Openly worshipped. Before, she'd been dealing with boys. Ike Drake was a grown-ass man. And she was becoming more and more attracted to the very type of man she claimed not to like.

Her cell phone rang. She thought about not answering it, but when she saw her grandmother's face, she gladly took the call. The chat was brief, but enough for her to get it together and stop acting like the scarecrow who needed a brain. She ended the call just as Ike pulled up to the country club valet.

They entered and were quickly ushered to a small, private dining room. Quinn knew it was one of five in the clubhouse, including the actual restaurant. After being seated she reached for her water, took a sip and presented Ike with a smile.

"I was a bit distracted earlier and wanted you to know that I really appreciate this invitation and the opportunity for us to talk under less combative circumstances."

"Absolutely. At the end of the day, there are hopefully no hard feelings. The accident and everything connected to it wasn't personal. It was business." Ike continued, his tone one of an executive in a corporate boardroom, "As is the core reason for this meeting. I understand that Lydia informed you that we're in the middle of closing on a major deal."

"Yes, she did. Congratulations."

"Thank you. It took several years to get to this point. That our company came out on top is a coup, given the competition. That is why the importance of everything handled from here on out cannot be overstressed."

"The former Compliance National building, correct? East of Kearny?"

Ike's brow creased. "Lydia told you that?"

Quinn shook her head. "I read it on some of the material I copied."

"The paperwork you filled out contained a confidentiality clause, which prohibits your discussing Drake business with anyone not directly connected to the company. You do understand that."

Quinn had never mastered patience and had little tolerance for elitist BS. "Yes, Ike, I'm familiar with the word and know what it means. Although I don't understand your reaction. A deal like this doesn't take place behind closed doors. Every real estate company in San Francisco probably knows about it, not to mention the companies that were beat out."

"Obviously," Ike responded, his displeasure apparent. "My comment is regarding the details that you may learn during your stint with us. I'm not sure of your level of corporate experience, if any, and want to make sure you're clear on protocol.

"Again, this isn't personal and not meant to demean you. But there's too much at stake for any part of this process to be assumed or left to chance."

Quinn listened and wondered what had brought on the change. On the drive over, Ike had seemed relaxed, casual. Was even nice enough to ignore her brief weirded-out state. Now she had relaxed and here he sat behind a corporate mask. So far it was obvious they brought out the best in each other. Nothing could make a meal last longer than discomfort. At least she was hungry and knew the food would be good. Deciding to concentrate on that, she picked up the menu.

"It appears I've upset you. That wasn't my intent."

"I don't believe you were intentionally insulting, but yes, your comment was quite condescending. Perhaps you've heard the rumors about me. But I can assure you that I am much more than a pretty face."

"That's good to know. The next four weeks should go by quickly."

"I sure hope so," Quinn mumbled.

The waiter entered with the fresh rolls and homemade fruit compotes for which the establishment was known. Quinn quickly reached for one, slathered it with butter and jam, and took a healthy bite. The more time her mouth was filled with food, the less she'd have to talk to Ike. If they were to survive these next weeks without killing each other, less would be more indeed.

Chapter 9

An hour later Ike reached his office, closed the door and took a deep breath. While they'd managed to regain a semblance of cordiality by the time the entrées arrived, the first part of the luncheon had not gone as planned. In fact, it began to go awry as soon as Quinn came around the corner.

He'd been expecting an inappropriately dressed brat and instead saw a woman—poised, professional, and stunning in the simplest of ways. The fresh face almost devoid of makeup, framed by wisps of hair that had escaped the loosened chignon. He'd seen the hairstyle on Lydia, his mother and other women. It looked different on Quinn. She made it look classy and sexy, even a bit naughty, at the same time. Or maybe the naughtiness he saw was a simple reflection of his thoughts as they rode down the elevator. How at that moment he would have liked nothing more than to push the emergency button, stop between floors and slowly pull away the pin that held her hair captive. He could imagine her lush, thick curls falling around her shoulders, could see those doe-like, trusting yet somewhat impish eyes giving him a baleful look. He'd slip in for a kiss and plunder her mouth while relieving her of that formfitting blue dress. She didn't wear pantyhose, he'd noticed. Her bare legs were flawless. He imagined she wore a thong, which would make the tryst easy. He'd simply unzip his pants, push the small triangle of fabric aside and…

He angrily pushed off the wall and crossed the room. Two more seconds and he would have been standing in his executive corner office with a full-blown hard-on. Wouldn't that have been a fine how-do-you-do? He wasn't some snot-nosed teenager experiencing his first crush. He was part owner of a successful real estate company, who'd dated some of the finest, most intelligent women the West Coast had to offer. His ex Audrey was one of them. They'd dated off and on for almost a decade, and Ike knew one thing for sure—Audrey had never made him feel the way he did right now after a somewhat acrimonious luncheon with Quinn.

Hearing a light tap on the door, he made a beeline for his desk and sat down quickly, just as Lydia opened the door. The thought of what she might have seen had he allowed his train of thought to reach the station left him feeling horrified.

"You all right, boss?"

"I'm fine." He picked up one of several folders strewn across his desk and browsed its contents. Not giving Lydia his full attention was a silent way he'd developed to convey that he was busy and didn't want to be bothered. The sound of her plopping down in the chair facing his desk was a clear indication that his message had not been received.

"Can't you see I'm busy?"

"I can see you're acting like it. I know you too well, Ike Drake. And while you're my boss and the way I make a living, you're also the kid I used to bully when I was twelve and you were seven."

Ike gave up the ruse and leaned back in the chair. "Yeah, you had about a foot on me then. Good thing my dad taught me manners. Otherwise three years and several inches later I would have doled out some serious payback."

"So?"

"So what?"

"So how did it go, the luncheon with Quinn? I like her!"

Ike shrugged, went back to reading. "It went all right."

"All right," she repeated sarcastically. "Dressed to the nines and a college graduate? Tell me you weren't impressed."

"I knew she'd graduated college."

"Did you know it was with dual degrees, Master's in both business management and international relations?"

"No. I didn't know that."

"She absolutely did, and she was modest about it. Earlier, I asked if she graduated college. She just said yes but didn't go into detail. She also graduated at the top of her class."

The shocked look on Ike's face made words unnecessary.

"Uh-huh. I thought that would get your attention."

"I can't deny that I'm surprised."

"Beautiful and smart, too. Doesn't seem fair. I'd be jealous if it would do any good."

"Where'd she go to college?"

"That's a good question, Ike. You should ask her."

"Wait, if she didn't tell you all this, how do you know?"

Lydia spoke quickly as she stood and went for the door. "My, oh, my, would you look at the time. That memo you need isn't going to type itself. I'd best be going."

"Lydia…" Ike warned.

She'd escaped his office but stuck her head in. "Don't forget your appointment with Jim is in an hour."

"While you're out there, type out your termination papers."

She laughed. "You know this office wouldn't function without me."

No one was indispensable, not even Ike. Yet what Lydia had said was more truth than fiction. She was an extremely talented assistant with stellar organizational skills and a near photographic memory. She was loyal, trustworthy, a lifelong friend whom he respected. But that didn't mean that she sometimes wasn't also an ulcer-causing irritant who warranted the occasional scolding. Ike loved her to pieces and was glad for her levity. It allowed him a cover for how uncomfortable her carefully and strategically dropped morsels of information had made him. Morsels she knew would pique his interest in a woman he'd denied any interest in.

Out, damned spot!

Ike tossed the paperwork aside and walked to a panel of windows that took up most of the corner office's back wall. Drake Realty Plus was situated on a piece of prime real estate in Paradise Cove's tony downtown, a corner lot of buildings that covered a quarter acre. Five stories high at its zenith, it was one of the town's taller buildings, reaching as high as city ordinances allowed. The executive offices were on the fifth floor. They offered pristine views of downtown and the mountains to the north and Paradise Valley's vast plains—including his brother Warren's thriving vineyard—farms and a new strip of businesses to the south. Ike's corner office afforded him the ability to see portions of both views, ones he'd often take in to help clear his head or focus on which business decision was best for both company and client. Today, however, clarity eluded him. There were several important matters that required his focus. Yet his mind was filled with thoughts of Quinn and an inexplicable attraction toward her that could no longer be denied. It was also one that couldn't be acted upon or publicly acknowledged. Which made Ike sure of at least one more thing—it was going to be a long month.

He left his desk and headed down the hall to Terrell's office, walked in and closed the door.

Terrell looked up from his laptop. When Ike closed the door, he sat back in his chair. "What's up, man? Did you read the last report for U Capital?"

"Did you know that Quinn has a college degree?" Ike perched on the edge of Terrell's desk.

"Sure, I knew it. Dual degrees, in business or finance or something like that. Graduated from Columbia." Terrell resumed work on his laptop. "Move, man!"

Ike got up. "Why didn't you tell me?"

"I tried. You weren't interested."

"When?"

"Or maybe I just started to tell you, but didn't after I

heard that you were unimpressed. Thought she was too young, immature, yada yada. From what I saw the other day, looks like you've changed your mind."

"What you saw wasn't as it appeared. Stay on track. When did I say that about her?"

"I don't know. Ask Warren. That's who told me."

After a light knock Warren walked in, as if on cue.

Ike started right in. "When did I talk to you about Quinn?"

Warren chuckled. "Damn, bro. That woman's got you bent!"

Terrell laughed, too. "Right."

"To hell with both of you," Ike grumbled.

"Don't get mad at me," Warren said. "You haven't been right since she hit your car. And the accident has nothing to do with what I'm talking about."

"If you'll remember, I hit my head."

Terrell glanced over. "So you're blaming your fixation on a head injury? Good try, Ike. Look, put yourself out of misery and ask the girl out."

"Considering the lunch we just had, that's not likely."

"You took her to lunch?"

"For business purposes."

Warren groaned. "Oh, here we go."

"Seriously. An orientation."

"For a four-week internship." Terrell was not convinced.

"During our biggest close ever. So yes, her understanding of protocol and this job's importance had to be confirmed."

"So what happened?" Warren asked.

"I said something she considered insulting. In hindsight, I agree."

"All the more reason to ask her to dinner. Sometimes making up is the best part. Now, unless you two are staying to discuss Ten Drake Plaza, I need my office back."

Warren held up his tablet opened to an Excel graph. "That's the only reason I'm here."

"Then let's get down to business." Terrell tapped his computer to life.

"It's about time," Ike said, taking a seat next to Warren. "Instead of going off on fantastical tangents, you two need to focus on the deal."

Chapter 10

The next morning, Quinn arrived at Drake Realty Plus ten minutes early. As she approached Lydia's desk on the way to the file room, it was obvious that the talkative executive assistant had gotten there much earlier. Lydia was on the phone but smiled and held up a finger, a silent signal for Quinn to wait. She stopped and observed what looked to be a whirlwind of activity. Several projects in various stages of completion were scattered across Lydia's desk. Folders, some bulging with files and other content, covered the credenza behind the desk. The inbox was full, a large mug of coffee nearly empty. Lydia continued to chat, typing information into the computer as she talked.

"That's already done, Ike, and on your desk. No, your dad hasn't yet signed off on it. As soon as it comes back, I'll have it couriered over to the bank." She switched to another screen. "There's the ten o'clock with Mr. Langston and...okay, push that back?" Her fingers flew across the keys. "No problem. I'll call and change that to a luncheon meeting at the club. Don't forget the conference call with GOE is at one. Ike, stop worrying and let me get back to work. I'll have the revisions on the report done by the time you get back. Okay, see you then."

She ended the call. "Good morning! Don't you look cute? Is that a skirt?" She stood and came from behind the desk.

"No, they're wide-legged pants."

"Gosh, I could never wear those things. I'd look like a whale. They look fab on you, though. And I see you wore shoes with a lower heel. Good girl."

"Spending all day in the file room definitely called for a different wardrobe. So I took your advice and went casual."

"Honey, I don't know that anything could look casual on you."

"Thanks but if you ever saw me lounging around the house in shorts and a tee, you'd change your mind."

The phone rang again. "Oh, darn. Give me just a sec, I need to ask you something." Lydia answered the call. "Ike Drake's office, Lydia speaking. Could you hold a moment, please?" She looked at Quinn. "What are you doing for lunch?"

"No special plans, why?"

"I'd like us to go together, if that's okay. I need your help with something."

"Sure, what time?"

"Eleven thirty. I know that's early, but I need to be here when Ike gets back."

"That's fine."

Two and a half hours later, Quinn and Lydia headed for the parking lot.

"I'll give you fair warning," Lydia said, having segued from one topic to another without taking a breath. "My car's a mess."

"I'll drive." Quinn took a right down the first row of cars and pointed her fob at a white Corvette.

"This is your car?"

"A rental, actually. My car won't be ready for another week."

"Oh, right. The accident, I forgot. Wow, fancy schmancy," Lydia exclaimed as she got in. "I thought it belonged to one of the salesmen. Would never have suspected a woman drove a Corvette. Not that there's anything wrong with it, of course."

"I was seven years old when I saw my first one, my dad's. It's always been my favorite car. So, where are we headed for lunch?"

"Cove Plaza, if you don't mind. There are a couple choices over that way—Acquired Taste and a new Mexican restaurant I've been wanting to try."

"Works for me." Quinn started the car and headed toward the strip mall.

"The main reason I want to go there, and why I asked you to lunch, is because there's a clothing store over that way, too, and I want to buy something to wear to Mr. Drake's birthday party. Not my boss, the elder."

"His birthday is coming up?"

Lydia nodded. "September seventeenth. Every year he throws a company party to celebrate it. You'll enjoy it. They're lots of fun."

"I don't think I'll be going. I'm not an employee."

"Not technically, perhaps, but you're still invited. Temps, interns, important clients, vendors—everyone comes out. In the past they've held them at the country club, but this year it will be at their center."

"Their center?"

"Yes, the Drake Community Center. It's mainly an educational and activity center for kids, but the auditorium is often rented out by different groups and organizations. And there's a big room that can convert to a large dining area that's used a lot, too. You're obviously not from here."

"No. I was born in Maryland and lived in San Francisco after my father relocated."

"What brought you here?"

"Life." When Lydia looked over questioningly, Quinn continued. "I was engaged to a…guy with a high profile and broke things off right before the wedding. It created a scandal, negative attention that my dad abhors, and another in what he considers a long list of my transgressions. I came here to hide out but am glad I did. My grandmother is getting older. It's better that she not live alone."

"If you don't mind me asking, why'd you break up with your fiancé?"

"He was a serial cheater. I never should have accepted his proposal."

"Well, if you're interested, the man you're working for is an eligible bachelor and a really super nice guy."

"Thanks, but no thanks. I probably won't get married at all—doubt there's a man out there who can be faithful."

"They're out there, Quinn. So try to stay open. You're much too pretty to spend life alone."

They pulled into the mall's parking lot. "Shop first or food first?" Quinn asked.

"I'd like to find something to wear first, unless you're real hungry."

"No, we can shop."

"Oh, by the way, there's an event this Saturday at the club, a golf outing. My husband fancies himself a pro on par with the Tiger Woods and Phil Mickelsons of the world. He's probably not even good enough to be their caddy, but I allow him the fantasy. You should come. It's for a worthy cause."

"I used to play a lot of golf," Quinn responded. "But I don't know about that. Small towns are huge gossip mills. I've no doubt that after the Days of Paradise ball, I'm the topic of many conversations."

"Who cares? People are going to talk. They have nothing better to do. I say let them and keep living your life."

"Will you be there?"

"Absolutely. Not because I'm crazy about the game, and I won't be playing, but a chance to spend some weekend time with grown-ups instead of three rambunctious kids!"

"I'll think about it."

She did, and after a week when from time to time Lydia mercifully delivered Quinn from the file room to help with other projects, Quinn agreed to attend the golf event. At the last minute, she decided to play and registered online Friday night. It was the first week of September, with the last of this summer's brilliance on full display. Vibrant flowers. Clear blue skies. A perfect seventy-seven degrees. With her regular golf clothes packed away, Quinn had hurriedly ordered appropriate attire from one of her favorite online stores. Nothing fancy or too outlandish—Quinn wanted to show the country club crowd that while she enjoyed the extreme, as was evident in her choice for the ball, she could also be fashionably restrained.

The event started at ten. She arrived at nine forty-five and was surprised to find the parking lot already full. After parking in an adjacent lot handling the overflow, she grabbed the bag of borrowed clubs from the trunk and her grandmother's visor and hurried into the club. Two seconds after signing in and getting her packet of information, she heard a voice behind her.

"What are you doing here?"

The tone of the question irked her—part irritation, part surprise.

She turned around and became even more annoyed. This time it was at her heartbeat, and how rapidly it accelerated, as she took in his look. Stark white shirt and slacks that highlighted his tan and dark brown eyes. Even the stern way he glowered looked sexy. He made her feel vulnerable and out of control. It was a feeling she didn't like, and she disliked him for making her feel it.

"Is there a reason I shouldn't be here?"

"Of course not. That probably didn't come out the way it sounded. I'm just surprised to see you, that's all. And with clubs. So you're playing?"

"Yes, but don't be scared. I won't beat you too badly." She walked around him and headed toward the patio near the first hole and where the tournament would begin. Walking away, she could feel his eyes on her. She tried to feel disgusted, told herself his behavior was typical of a man. But truthfully, it made her feel good. She wasn't ready to admit that her feelings toward him were shifting. Couldn't accept that she'd ever find a man who reminded her of her father attractive. But Ike wasn't her father. And today, he looked finer than ever.

The tournament began. Quinn was competitive and soon was focused solely on making each hole. But Ike's heat was just ahead of hers. She observed his game and couldn't help but admire his swing. Or his long, strong legs. Or how nicely his buns filled out the slacks.

A nice-looking jerk, she reminded herself, one who'd sued her and acted out of her league. Her temporary boss. She was glad for the reminder of why liking or dating him was out of the question. She was in this for the duration of her penalty, not a day longer, and couldn't wait for the ordeal to be over.

Chapter 11

"Quinn! Wait up!"

For the second time today, Quinn heard a familiar voice from behind her. She turned around, shielding her eyes from the sun as Ike came toward her. Across the street, she noticed a woman watching intently. His girlfriend, perhaps? No, she decided. Men could do stupid things but surely he wouldn't be that dumb.

"You held your own," he said when he reached her. "Good job."

"Not as good as you. Until you found the sand trap on the fourteenth hole, I thought you might win it all."

"Your car over here?"

"Yep."

"I'll walk you to it."

The offer surprised Quinn, but she simply nodded and turned toward the lot.

"You're pretty good."

"I used to be, but it's been a while since I played. Which was clearly evident today."

"No, I was watching your swings, how you addressed the shot. I could tell it wasn't your first time on the green. Or the second. Why'd you quit?"

"Seriously? Double bogies back to back? Competing against guys like you? It was easier to simply make a donation to the cause and watch from the comfortable shade of the patio. So that's what I did."

They reached Quinn's car. She tapped the key fob and opened the trunk. Ike took her clubs and placed them inside.

"Why are you being nice to me?"

"Placing your golf clubs in the trunk?" He shrugged. "I'm a gentleman."

"You're a jerk, remember?"

Ike smiled. Quinn noticed. She hadn't seen him do that often and decided he should. It gave him a younger, more carefree appearance. "We're back to that again. Because I sued for the repairs."

"That, too, but right now because you'd choose to leave your girlfriend stranded to be a gentleman to me."

"Who are you talking about?"

"Don't look now, but she's behind you, across the street. Her face is familiar, but I don't know her name. She obviously knows you, and probably quite well."

"What does she look like?"

"Tall, slender, shoulder-length brown hair. Do you know who I'm talking about?"

"Probably. In a small town, everybody knows everybody. But I don't have a girlfriend, and I am not a jerk."

"Okay. Thanks for the help. I'll see you Monday."

She walked to the car door. Three long strides and he'd passed her and opened the door. "Where are you going?"

"Home. Before I get arrested."

"For what?"

"Driving illegally. Thanks to you, my license is still restricted. If I get caught between here and home, I might go to jail."

"Then there's only one way to handle this."

Quinn's eyes narrowed. "How?"

"I have to follow you."

"Ha! No, thanks. That won't be necessary."

"You may not think so, but that's what's going to happen."

"We'll see." Quinn huffed and got into her car. *Who does this guy think he is?*

She started her car. Ike pulled out his phone, did a quick scroll and tapped the screen. She put the car in reverse. He placed a hand on the door.

"Yes, is this the Paradise Cove police department? I may need to report a driving violation." He eyed her with a look that read, *Can you hear me now?*

"Seriously?"

Ike smiled again, that lazy, fun spread of perfectly plump lips revealing sparkly white teeth. "Seriously."

She threw the gear in Park and crossed her arms.

He laughed out loud. "Wait here."

"Such an asshole," she muttered as he walked away.

He stopped and turned around. "What did you say?"

"You obviously heard me."

"You're really angry."

"Of course I am! I know you Drakes think this town belongs to you, but when I entered the city limits the sign read Paradise Cove, not Drake Town."

"Quinn, do you think I'd actually call the cops on you? I was teasing. I'm usually quite adept at sharing my ideas, thoughts and concepts, but for some reason comments made to you are misinterpreted. I know we got off to a bad start and I want to fix that. So what I did was a way to, you know, spend some time together."

This long explanation earned him an equally long look. "In that case, if spending time with me is what you wanted, you should have simply asked."

"Oh. Okay. Ms. Taylor, would you do me the honor of spending time with me this evening?"

She offered her best smile as she put her car in gear. "No."

When Quinn chanced a glance in the rearview mirror, two people caught her eye. Ike, who stood with hands on hips and watched her exit. And the tall, slender woman crossing over to where he stood.

Quinn told herself she didn't care about whatever was taking place in her rearview mirror. Men were the last thing on her mind. That much was true. As she went to sleep that night, she thought of Ike.

It seemed Monday mornings were coming much too quickly, and too often. He should have been exhausted, but the progress made so far toward closing on Ten Drake Plaza and his unexpected time on the course with Quinn had invigorated a part of him that he was sure had not been invigorated before. The final piece of good news had been the text he'd received from the car repairman late last night. A part that before had taken more than a year to find before had been found through the internet. As soon as its availability was authenticated, Ike's mechanic could forward the purchase information to Quinn's attorney.

Quinn. The woman had stayed on his mind all weekend long. The very thing that initially turned him off now totally tantalized him. Her spunk and total disregard for propriety gave life an edge he'd never experienced and didn't think he cared for. Something about her made a part of him wake up that he hadn't known slept. He'd thought he knew what he wanted in a woman. Now he was willing to concede that perhaps he was just finding out.

He headed straight to the break room nearest his office. A shot of espresso was in order. He smelled the coffee from a good ten feet away. Obviously Lydia and he had shared the same idea. The early bird not only got the worm but closed the deal.

"Tweet, tweet, my swe… Quinn!"

Quinn laughed in spite of herself. "Obviously not who you were expecting."

He decided that if Quinn could smile 24/7, the world wouldn't need the sun. "No, I thought it was Lydia. She usually gets here early."

"Yes, she's on her way."

"She called?"

Quinn shook her head. "No. She told me at the tournament that she'd be late. I'm in to cover for her."

"She should have gotten one of the assistants to cover for her. Not that there's anything wrong with you," he added, all too aware of how often his words were misconstrued. "But you're here as part of a court order, and not getting paid. So there's no need to work extra hours."

"I'm not. I'll leave an hour early."

"Okay, good." He walked over to the cupboard, pulled out a mug boasting the company logo and filled it with flavored coffee. The shot of espresso was no longer needed. Seeing Quinn had given his mind, body and spirit an energy boost. "She gave you her card key, too?"

"No. Your brother Terrell and I arrived at the same time."

"Terrell's here?" Ike looked at his watch. "Wonders never cease. It actually works out that you're here early. I'd like to discuss a couple things with you."

Quinn turned and leaned on the counter and eyed him warily. "Okay."

"Why the leery look? It's nothing bad. Come on. Let's go into my office."

They stepped into the spacious, immaculate space. Once inside, he closed the door. Quinn stopped and turned around, her look distrustful.

"Quinn, what is it? If I make you that uncomfortable, we can keep it open. I closed it to keep our discussion private. But if it makes you feel in any way uneasy..."

"Is this about Saturday and my turning you down?"

Ike's eyes lit up with understanding. Hearing the source of her angst, he took a relieved breath. Maybe she didn't think he was the big bad wolf after all. Before her time with the company was over, he planned to convince her he wasn't a jerk, either.

"No, this isn't about what happened on Saturday," he answered, walking by her to the comfy sitting area on the other side of the room. "Though your abrupt departure was very impolite. It left me in the dust, literally. Let's sit over here. It's more casual."

He sat on the love seat. She sat on one of two roomy armchairs, upholstered with a velvety textured chenille of striped, warm fall colors.

"First of all, Lance received the paperwork from your attorney, and the repair shop was given the address to send the invoices. Thank you."

"You're welcome."

"Unfortunately, this process is going to take time. The parts are few and rare, but I'll make sure you're kept up-to-date through your attorney."

"Okay."

"I seem to have had to do this quite a bit with you, but I need to apologize to you, once again. I assumed something about you that isn't true."

"What, that I'm not the spoiled, rich brat the rumor mill has labeled me, and that you, too, believe?"

"I never said that."

"You never used those words. But from the moment our cars collided, you made it clear that my reckless, irresponsible ways were to blame. Unfortunately, the dog that I'm positive ran in front of my car obviously vanished into thin air, which only underscores that incorrect belief."

"Duly noted." He paused to take a sip of coffee, continue to look at her. She stared back. Direct. Fearless.

Damn, she was sexy when she got fired up. Ike dared not imagine how that fire translated in the bedroom. Not if he wanted to continue this meeting and preserve his dignity.

"Of course there has been talk about you. That's what people in small towns do when someone new arrives. Speculate, gossip, try to figure out who or what you're about. Especially someone who makes the type of entrance you did, showing up at a charity ball in such scanty attire."

"I was fully covered, thank you."

"In the front. But in the back, you could have sneezed and been arrested for indecent exposure."

"It may have appeared that way, but trust me, that is not the case. So while I may not have been covered from head to toe, there was coverage in all the places that mattered. As for how people felt about what I wore, that's none of my business."

"You don't care what people think about you?"

"Everyone wants to be liked. That's only natural. But when you grow up as I did, and get talked about and lied about as much as I have, you stop defending or explaining yourself and grow a thick skin."

"The first day we had lunch and I mentioned your duties, among other things, why didn't you tell me you had two master's degrees?"

"You didn't ask. As I said the other day, you assumed I was just a pretty face. And a spoiled, rich one at that."

"Was I correct in hearing that one of your degrees is in in business administration?"

"Yes."

"What career are you pursuing?"

"I'm still figuring that out."

"How old are you, if you don't mind me asking?"

"Twenty-five."

"I figured you were about the same age as my younger sister." He reared back, eyes toward the ceiling as he began to recollect. "By the time I was your age, I'd worked full-time for...let's see...almost five years. That includes the two years I was getting my master's degree. You've still got time, but don't wait too long. The older you get, the faster time flies."

"How old are you?"

"Thirty-five."

"Oh."

Ike paused. "What do you mean, oh?"

"I thought you were older."

The scowl that formed was a hint that Ike was none too pleased with this perception.

"I don't mean that in a bad way. I just… You act older, that's all. The way you just spoke to me, for instance, with all of this sage wisdom for a young 'un like me." She adopted a low, gravelly tone at the end of the sentence, sounding much like her father.

"I didn't sound like that."

"No, that was a bad impression of my father."

"Glen Taylor."

"You know him?"

"I've met him. He played a tournament at the club several years ago. My dad knows him better, though. Says they once served on a committee together. Judge Taylor seems to be the no-nonsense type, very disciplined. I was surprised to learn that you're his daughter."

Quinn sighed, took a few sips of tea as she looked out the window. "Why, because his life resembles a sturdy oak, while mine is more that of a leaf blowing in the wind?" He didn't answer. "We're alike in ways that aren't obvious. I feel I've never had the chance to ponder my future freely, with no expectations. To get to know myself well enough to discover who I am and what I truly like. Besides fast cars, strong men and hot…tea."

Her eyes danced as they viewed him over the rim of the mug holding her citrus-flavored concoction. It warmed his heart to see her relaxed. The way she teased him warmed other places.

"You didn't have the chance because of the way you grew up? Is that part of getting the thick skin you mentioned? Again, I don't mean to get too personal here, and if you'd rather not answer it's fine."

"I don't mind at all. I'd rather be asked directly and have the opportunity to replace hearsay with facts. Along with the no-nonsense, disciplined traits you recognized, I'm the only child of a very commanding, stubborn and opinionated man."

"Qualities that undoubtedly helped make him a successful attorney and respected judge."

"I can't deny that. He's an excellent businessman. Those same traits don't work so well as a dad."

"I can understand that."

"It was stifling. I'm a lot like him, so growing up was often…combative. But since he's successful, as you say, a very good debater and negotiator, it became easier to agree with his suggestions rather than argue against them. So when I reached my senior year still undecided about a major, he determined that Columbia was a great college and that business admin was a multipurpose degree. Which is where I went and what I received."

"Are he and your mom still on good terms?"

Ike was immediately sorry that he'd asked the question. The shadow that crossed her eyes was as intense as clouds covering the sun before a downpour.

"Never mind. We don't have to talk about it."

"No. It's all right." Quinn swallowed the sadness that made her throat constrict and batted away the tears. "My grandmother says that in doing so…she continues to live. My mom was… I lost her just before I turned twelve. Her name was Brenda."

"I'm sorry," Ike replied as Quinn quickly swiped a lone tear. "No doubt she was beautiful, just like you."

He watched her grapple with a myriad of thoughts, saw her jaw tense with the effort to not cry. "Thank you."

Later he would realize that it was this very moment, when the flippant, fiery spoiled brat faded away and he saw the vulnerable, frightened little girl inside her, that he fell in love with Quinn Taylor.

Quinn looked at her watch. "I should probably go to Lydia's desk and review how to take the phones off night service. It sounded easy enough, but she said the instructions are in her drawer. I want to find them just in case."

"Don't worry about that. The service will handle them. We still haven't gotten to why I brought you in here."

He got up, walked over to his desk and returned with a report elegantly bound in a faux-leather cover. He handed it to her.

She read the title aloud. "'San Francisco Financial District: An Analysis of Growth Projection, Market Demand, Infrastructure and Capacity.'"

Beneath the title was a subheading that tied the overall report more specifically to the Compliance National Bank Building in downtown San Francisco.

"A study conducted on the building you're buying," she affirmed while flipping through the pages. "Looks quite comprehensive."

"We believe so."

She looked up. "So what about this do you want to discuss with me?"

"I don't know. But hearing of your degree in business administration made me curious as to what your thoughts on the report would be."

"You want me to read this?"

"On company time, of course. I'll talk to Lydia and if necessary get someone else in to handle what you were doing."

"Who did the study?" Quinn turned back to the front of the report. Ike told her. "Hmm. I've not heard of them, but that doesn't necessarily mean anything."

"The company was recommended by our partners."

"Oh, so this purchase is in partnership with other companies."

"Only one, Global 100, and it's a silent partnership."

He watched her brows furrow as she flipped through the document. "I don't know what I could possibly add, but sure. I'd be happy to look over it."

"I'd appreciate it."

"Do you have a time frame that you'd like to have my response?"

"I'm not expecting you to read it cover to cover, all of the tables and graphs. They're rather tedious. Just a general perusal of the main sections, so maybe a couple of days."

"No problem." She stood up. "I'll get right to it."

Ike's phone rang. He looked at the ID. "Hey, Dad." He nodded as Quinn gave a quick wave goodbye and headed out of his office. She looked as good going as she did coming, no doubt about that. He was quickly discovering that the more he found out about Quinn Taylor, the more he wanted to know.

Chapter 12

Quinn sat at her grandmother's dining room table, picking over a salad as she read the report Ike had given her. She hadn't been too excited when he'd asked her to read it, but after digging in she'd become enthralled. Learning had always been a fun experience, even subjects that weren't particularly exciting. It had been a long time since she'd had to use the type of analytical and comprehensive skills that work like this required. To do so felt better than she could have imagined.

She'd bypassed the tedious number-filled pages on profit and projections and instead homed in on infrastructure and capacity. San Francisco proper had run out of available land long before Quinn was born. Office space went for a premium, with waiting lists of several years. Those who were lucky enough to own buildings usually hung on to them. She found it a bit odd that a structure this profitable and strategically located would be up for sale. Of course it hardly mattered what she thought. Drake Realty Plus was a highly successful company that had negotiated hundreds if not thousands of transactions. A company didn't become that successful without knowing their stuff.

Her phone rang. She looked at the screen and smiled. "Hello, Trench Coat!" She pushed the speaker button and headed to the kitchen with her empty salad bowl. "What's up, Trent?"

"Nothing much. What are you doing?"

"Working."

"Get out of here."

"Ha! I'm serious. I'm putting my Ivy League education to work."

"Doing what?"

Quinn told him.

"Global 100? Are you sure?"

"Positive. Why are you asking in that tone?"

"Who is their contact and how well do they know him?"

"I don't have a name, and even if I did couldn't share it. Confidential company information. Even mentioning the partnership may have been out of line."

"Seriously? You're saying that to me?"

"I'm just mentioning it as a reminder to myself. Now tell me what you know about them."

"It's rumored that the backbone of their financing capabilities is a group of nefarious, corrupt businessmen and politicians with access to their countries' coffers. They use the funds to increase their already ridiculous wealth while the citizens starve and the country goes bankrupt."

"No way."

"They're ruthless, all about the dollar. Dad stopped doing business with them years ago, before he retired."

"That's right! Your dad was the president of Compliance National at one time. How did I not remember that?"

"I don't know."

Quinn stood and paced the room. "If what you say is true, why are people still doing business with them? Why isn't this public knowledge? Why didn't your dad report them to someone?"

"Um, maybe because he prefers his head without a bullet hole in it?"

"He was threatened?"

"I don't know what they did or said, but he's never talked about it, and he's not the only one who knows. Besides, stuff like that is hard if not impossible to prove. Heck, I can't even say for sure it's true. It might be as Global tried to tell Dad...just a rumor."

"Great, get me all worked up over something that might be make-believe."

"Hey, I'm just sayin'."

"Well, I wish you hadn't."

"Then forget it. Just be happy that you're doing something interesting."

"It beats filing and making photocopies for eight hours a day."

"I hear that."

"Plus, I'm getting to know Ike a little better. We're not stark enemies anymore."

"Who?"

"Ike Drake."

"The dude who sued you? The jerk?" Quinn laughed. "He's not a jerk anymore, huh. You must have let him hit it."

"I did not. That's such a guy answer. Enough about me. How's the project with your uncle? When are you coming back this way?"

"Probably not for a couple weeks."

"You've got to be here for Halloween, and the masquerade ball. I texted you about it, and you agreed to attend it with me."

"I want to, but I can't leave until we close on this house."

"That's what your uncle wanted?"

"Yep. Waterfront property on Martha's Vineyard."

"You're kidding. I know someone who's been trying to buy a place there for, like, ever!"

"It's not on the side you're talking about, but in an area called Oak Bluffs."

"It's part of Martha's Vineyard? Never heard of it."

"I hadn't, either. The area has an interesting history. During segregation it was an enclave for the black elite. Doctors, lawyers, celebrities, politicians, and all black-owned. But the newer generations who've inherited the properties aren't as interested in keeping them, or maybe can't afford it. Right now, the prices are sweet. So I'm going to check out a couple properties. If you weren't on lockdown, I'd ask you to fly over."

"Negative, friend. I still have a week or so of jail time."

"You don't sound unhappy. I think it's because you're doing Warden Ike."

"Very funny. I told you, nothing's happening there. He's not my type, but he is kind of handsome, in that buttoned-up businessman sort of way."

"He's gone from a jerk to handsome in two weeks? The guy doesn't stand a chance."

"Just go buy your houses and get back over this way. I want you to meet him."

Quinn ended the call. She couldn't stop smiling. Trent was right. He knew her too well. She was beginning to catch feelings for the warden and wonder how efficiently he used his baton. Then she thought about what Trent had shared about Global 100. The smile faded.

Three days later, Quinn left the cubicle she now occupied and walked toward Ike's office. His door was closed.

"Lydia, hi."

"Oh, hi, Quinn. How's it going?"

"I'm fine. How are you doing?"

"Can't complain. I bet you're liking that workstation better than the file room."

"A lot better. But my stay there may be over."

"Is that the report Ike gave you?"

Quinn nodded. "Is he here?"

"Yes, but he's on the phone. A conference call. I can give it to him for you unless you need to discuss it with him."

"He might have questions. If so, let me know."

"Will do. And don't worry. I won't put you back in the dungeon." She looked around her crowded desk and at the credenza. "Tell you what. How good a typist are you?"

"I can type."

"Are you familiar with Excel?"

"Yes, basically."

"I have a bunch of information that needs to be transferred to the computer but I probably should set up the chart first. It's too early for lunch, but why don't you take a break, let me get this together and then I'll bring it to you."

"Or I can go to lunch if you want. I was thinking of trying out the little sandwich shop down the street."

"The deli? Oh, you'll like it. The food's good there. The owner's nice, too."

Lydia was right. The owner took Quinn's order and made her feel so welcome she ate her meal there. She returned to learn that Ike had wanted to speak with her but the execs had gone to lunch. Lydia showed Quinn the charts she'd set up and soon Quinn was busy inputting the information. The afternoon flew by, and when she left at five, speaking with Ike had slipped her mind, along with her trepidation about doing so.

The relief was short-lived. In every idle moment, her thoughts returned to Global 100. She found it hard to believe a family like the Drakes, who appeared to be good, upstanding citizens, would do business with anyone shady. Yet it was equally difficult to imagine someone as thorough and detailed as Ike would not know everything about a company before doing business with them.

My dad...liked his head without the bullet hole.

Then again, maybe he didn't know. Maybe like everyone else, the Drakes were in the dark.

She neared home, dreading an evening with nothing to do but think. The original plans had called for Trent to be here by now. Working on the report had been mentally stimulating. With that project over and unwanted thoughts abounding, the ho-hum existence that had become her life was amplified. Small-town life was driving her crazy. So even though her license was still restricted, Quinn called Peyton with plans to head out of town.

She got voice mail, but after checking on her grandmother and relaying her plans, she headed for the Cove. Hopefully by the time she finished a glass of wine, Peyton would have returned her call.

Seconds later, her phone rang.

"Whose phone are you using?"

There was a brief pause. "Mine."

Quinn wasn't expecting a male voice, especially this one. "Ike?"

"You were obviously expecting someone else."

"Yes," she replied, pressing her hand against a heart that had begun to race. "I'd just called a friend and thought she was calling me back. How'd you get my number?"

"I asked Lydia. It was on the form you filled out before coming to work."

"Oh."

"Is this a bad time?"

Yes. No. "I don't know. What do you have in mind?"

The pause was longer this time. "Dinner."

"Seriously? You called to ask me out?"

"Actually, no, but your question demanded I think of something more exciting than discussing a report."

"We can do both. In fact, I'm headed to the Cove now. There's a restaurant over there."

"Acquired Taste."

"Yes, that's it."

"I'd actually prefer we meet at this place inside the Golden Gates community."

"What place is that?"

"My home."

"Oh." She drew out the word. "I get it."

He chuckled. "I'm sure you think you do, but I have no ulterior motives. I rarely eat out, because one, there's only so many times you can eat at the same restaurants, two, I know my way around a kitchen and three, for all of the small-town drawbacks we discussed the other day."

"Hmm."

"Don't feel pressured. It was a spontaneous invitation. Call me back after dinner and we can discuss it over the phone."

"Not so fast, Mr. Drake. Give a girl a chance to make you sweat a little."

"Oh, is that what you're doing?"

"Yes. Are you sweating?"

"Not hardly. And I may be old, but you may call me Ike."

"I thought you were going to say 'not yet,' Ike." Silence. "Don't feel pressured," she mimicked. "What's your address?"

He relayed it. "Any special preference for dinner? I can cook just about anything."

"And I eat just about everything. So surprise me."

Quinn changed the car's direction once again, this time toward the tiny community of Golden Gates. Her feelings ping-ponged between anxiety and excitement. Ike had invited her over to discuss work. She'd rather spend the evening forgetting about work, and she could imagine several different positions that would get the job done.

Chapter 13

After a quick scan of his walk-in pantry, Ike decided on a simple, all-in-one dish. He pulled a package of linguine from the shelf, vegetables from the fridge and seasonings from the cabinet. After turning on the stereo, he pulled out his chopping board, rolled up his sleeves and went to work. He found cooking therapeutic, relaxing and a great time to ponder. Some of his best decisions had come amid chopping, slicing and frying. When it came to Quinn and the feelings happening toward her, there was a lot to think about.

It had been a decade since he'd been single. He'd been with Audrey off and on since he was twenty-five. The same age as Quinn was now. Another long-term relationship lasted from his senior year of college through grad school. Ike was nobody's saint, but he'd never been a player, either. There was no judgment of people who were, but it wasn't in his nature. He loved fiercely and intensely and gave 200 percent to everything he did, including relationships. Before graduating high school, he'd already tired of playing the field.

Quinn. He'd never seriously dated anyone like her, was usually not attracted to gregarious, feisty women. He gravitated toward women like his mom and grandmother. Then he remembered that his mom had found Quinn delightful. Maybe he didn't know Jennifer Drake as well as he thought.

He diced fresh tomatoes, onions and garlic and began a simple marinara sauce. What would a relationship with Quinn look like? Did they have enough in common to sustain spending a lot of time together? Heck, for that matter, did they have anything in common at all? He reached for fresh herbs—rosemary, thyme and basil—and placed them in a chopper. A couple pulses and they were ready to be added to the skillet where the diced vegetables now cooked down in olive oil. Ike was a workaholic and proud of it. When he wasn't working, he liked chilling at home. Quinn was an extrovert, a social butterfly from what he'd seen. It was a popular belief that opposites attract. Ike believed that to be true. But did they date, marry and stay together for life?

The chiming doorbell told Ike Quinn had arrived. Just before opening the door, he stopped in front of a hallway mirror. Turned his head left to right and back again. *I don't look old. Do I?* Not one to ever have worried much about his looks, he shook off the self-conscious feeling even as he recalled his morning shave and an encounter with one gray hair. *Not old*, he told himself again. *Distinguished.*

"Hi, Quinn. Come on in."

"Thanks." She stepped inside, taking in the decor as they left the foyer and walked down a short hall. They turned right into a living room with two-story ceilings and huge windows that brought nature inside. "You have a very nice home. I love the windows." Walking farther into the room, she turned and asked him, "All of this for just you?"

"All by my lonesome."

"I'm sure that's not entirely true." She held out a bag. "With you fixing dinner, I figured I'd buy the wine."

"That wasn't necessary, but it was very nice of you. Thanks."

"I didn't know what you were fixing. I hope cabernet is okay."

"It's perfect. Come on back. We're having pasta, and it's not quite ready."

"You're inviting me into your kitchen? I don't know, Ike. I'm pretty much allergic to that room."

"You don't cook?" Quinn shook her head. "Anything?"

"Nothing."

"That's crazy."

"It's how I grew up. Dad always had a cook and then there was boarding school. At college there was a cook for our house. I guess it's my normal."

"Have a seat. Wait, first, can you get a couple wineglasses from that cabinet?" Quinn walked to where he'd pointed. "The wine opener is in the drawer beneath it, and yes, I'd like a glass."

"Okay." Quinn brought the glasses and bottle over to a grand island that dominated the kitchen. She sat on one of two stools on the side away from where Ike prepared dinner, and ran a hand over the shiny countertop. "This is beautiful, Ike. What is it?"

"Copper."

"Wow, nice. Granite or marble is almost all you see these days. I like that this is different."

"Thank you."

"How'd you discover that you liked cooking?"

"It started in college. Basic stuff that you opened and mixed. Frozen dinners. Microwave. At one point some friends and I moved into an apartment. The girl I dated at the time knew how to cook. I'd hang out with her while she was preparing dinner and little by little I'd pick things up. Over time I discovered I liked it."

"I never would have imagined you in the kitchen."

"What did you think of me initially, besides being a jerk?"

"I thought you were kind of geeky. I don't mean that in a bad way."

"I don't take that in a bad way. Geeks are some of the wealthiest, most successful people in the world."

"Then, when I saw you at the trial, in the suit, it was more the corporate businessman image. You remind me of my dad."

"Just his good qualities, right?"

"You wish, but, um, no."

"Ha! I was afraid that would be your answer."

"It's a certain air that many executives have. You're used to bossing people around and having things run the way you want them. Dad would do that at home as well as in the office. But since working at your company, I've seen other sides that aren't so bad."

"Gee, thanks."

"You're welcome. What about me? What are some of the rumors going around about me?"

"I don't hang out, per se, so I haven't heard a lot of them. One is that you were a runaway bride."

"That's the word, huh?"

"No, I'm exaggerating a bit. But it is being said that you broke up with a guy not long before the planned wedding."

"That's not rumor. That's truth. He wasn't who he said he was, and I wasn't going to lose myself just to save face."

"Good answer."

"What else?"

"You already know about the spoiled, rich part." Ike lowered the heat on the stove's contents, picked up his glass and leaned against the counter. "I'm less interested about rumor and more about who you really are."

"Okay. Shoot."

"Why did you move here?"

"To help my grandmother. She's dealing with a couple medical issues and needs support, of the moral kind, mainly. Another reason is the breakup. Planning the wedding was stressful—dealing with his family and protocol and the public facade was a lot. After the scandal of a public breakup, I needed to retreat from the spotlight. I'd forgotten how slow it is here, though. Not sure I can give Grandmother the year that I promised."

"You were living in Paris?"

"Yes."

"Paradise Cove is not Paris."

"At all."

"That's a huge change."

"Yes, it is. You've never thought of living somewhere else?"

"I like living here. Excitement, if I need it, is a plane ride away. Aside from work, mine is a fairly laid-back lifestyle. You probably can't imagine that."

"I'm getting a taste of it now."

"How do you like it so far?"

"Honestly? I'm about to go crazy."

Ike laughed out loud. "Well, there's no need to go there hungry. Food's ready. Let's eat."

After settling down at the table in the informal dining room, Quinn picked up the conversation. "I can't believe you cooked this, Ike. It's delicious."

"Thank you."

"Even the sauce tastes fresh."

"It is."

"You made the sauce?" He nodded. "I'm impressed. It's really good, like restaurant quality."

"I'm glad you're enjoying it."

Quinn took a couple more bites before stopping to sip some water. "You know my story. I'm the runaway bride. What about you? What, why are you smiling?"

"I was thinking earlier that we probably had nothing in common. But just now it hit me that I'm practically the runaway groom."

"You ended an engagement?"

"I ended a relationship that lasted for a very long time."

"Was it the woman at the golf tournament, the one watching our every move from across the street?"

"Yes. Her name is Audrey."

"How long were you two together?"

"Off and on for ten years."

"Jeez. That is a long time to discover that you don't like someone."

"It wasn't that. I like her just fine. I just didn't love her in the way I felt a husband should his wife."

"And what way is that?"

"Totally. Completely. Forever."

He said this and it was as if the air changed. Energy shifted. Quinn looked at him, absorbing the words, her wineglass half lifted to her mouth. The mouth grabbed his attention, her lips colored with the wine, slightly parted, just enough for his tongue to slip inside. Sounds of a sexy saxophone drifted across the table. The moment only lasted a few seconds. And forever at the same time.

"I'm curious to get your thoughts on the report."

"Report?"

"Yes, the one you came over to discuss?"

"Oh, yes, right. The report."

"You forgot."

Quinn's eyes traveled from his eyes to his lips and back. "For a moment, yes. I did."

What she hadn't forgotten was what Trent had shared about the Drakes' silent partner. Her mind was in turmoil over what to do. If she mentioned it, Ike would know that she'd discussed what was confidential with someone outside the company. If she remained silent, she'd never know whether or not the Drakes had made an informed choice to partner with criminals. Not now, she finally decided. She wasn't ready and needed more information.

Reaching for a napkin, she patted her lips and began. "Overall it seemed pretty standard. It appears the company did a very thorough job. I also pulled up a couple of similar reports online, not on the Compliance building, but on the financial district. The research results were pretty much all in line." She spent several minutes sharing thoughts on growth capacity and market strategies. "Regarding the Compliance National building, at least, your information is detailed, comprehensive and complete."

Ike nodded but said nothing.

"That's what you wanted, right—my take on the report?"

"Yes."

"Okay. You didn't say anything, so I wasn't sure."

"I was just absorbing what you said. Thank you. Those are some very valid observations." He peered at her closely. "Anything else?"

A moment's hesitation and then, "No. That's it."

"I appreciate your feedback."

"No problem."

"Were you that nervous about sharing your opinion? You seem relieved."

"No, reviewing the report was oddly enjoyable, with much I'd learned and thought forgotten coming back like that." She snapped her fingers.

"Good. Over the next couple weeks, I'll keep that in mind. In case there's more to review."

Conversation flowed much easier after that. Quinn accepted Ike's offer of gelato for dessert. Shortly after they finished it, her grandmother called.

"Gotta run?"

"Yes," Quinn answered, reaching for her purse and standing. "I'm sure she's wondered where I've been and will be full of questions."

"She's a good woman, your grandmother."

"Yes. She is."

They reached the front door.

"Thanks for dinner, Ike. It was really good. Your home is lovely and you're a fine host."

"It was my pleasure. Thanks for taking the time to read the report and share your findings."

"You're welcome. Could you ever have imagined that day after the wreck that I'd be in your home having a civil conversation?"

"Not at all. Just goes to show you…anything's possible."

He couldn't go another second without touching her. Reaching out, he pulled her into a warm yet brief embrace.

Any longer and his body would have made the fierce attraction he felt very clear. Watching her car pull out of his driveway, he knew one thing for sure—it wouldn't be the last time he held her.

Chapter 14

The next evening, Quinn arrived at the Drake Community Center for the company birthday dinner for Ike Drake Sr. While working at their office she'd mostly kept to herself, and now she felt a bit awkward attending a company event. The thought of being in a room full of Drakes was unnerving. What she'd withheld from Ike last night caused further stress. But after being reminded by both Ike and Lydia that her presence was expected, she had no choice but to spread her social butterfly wings and attend.

Lydia had also reminded her that clients, vendors and others would be there. So Quinn stepped into the center's expertly transformed dining area looking to see a familiar face. She did. Directly in her line of sight was an elegantly dressed and smiling Jennifer Drake, beckoning her forward.

"Jennifer," she said with outstretched hand. "How nice to see you again. I'm Margaret Newman's granddaughter, Quinn—"

"Taylor. I know who you are, Quinn Taylor. It's wonderful to see you, too, looking stunning as always."

"Thank you. I love that jumpsuit. It looks classy but comfy—reminds me of a Chai design."

Jennifer raised a brow. "Very good eye. I'm impressed. Not too many know of her. It's from her upcoming resort collection."

"How are you wearing it now?"

"Connections, darling." Jennifer winked and offered a wave to someone across the room. "One of my dear friends is related to Chai's husband. Every now and then she'll send me something she's whipped up, to get my feedback or just because. When this arrived, I loved it immediately and simply couldn't wait until spring to show it off."

"Nor should you. That shade of tan and the linen fabric works for every season of the year."

"A real fashionista. I knew when you walked into the ballroom that night that we'd get along."

Quinn made a face. "Ah, yes. My grand entrance into Paradise Cove."

Jennifer chuckled. "I must admit you made quite a splash. I assume that was your intention."

"The designer is a friend of mine and I love the dress. When I put it on, I thought it was hella sexy!" Jennifer laughed again. "But…this is a small town, mine is a new face and tongues wagged."

"That they did. Your attendance definitely added sizzle to what can sometimes be a rather stuffy affair."

"Always willing to do my part."

"How is your time at the company going? Is everyone treating you okay?"

"The time could go more quickly, but I have no complaints."

"Not cut out for the corporate life?"

"I'm not sure what I'm cut out for, besides causing controversy. I seem to be good at that."

"Sometimes a little controversy is the spice of life. Takes you out of your comfort zone. Lets you know what you're made of. Ah, here comes someone whose life could use a little shaking up." Jennifer waved at someone behind Quinn. "But not too much," she leaned forward and whispered. "His heart couldn't take it. Hi, darling."

Quinn turned as Ike reached them. "Hello, Mother." He pulled her into an embrace. "Good evening, Quinn."

"Hi, Ike." Quinn leaned in for a hug, as well. He caught her shoulders with his hands, tightened his arms to prevent her forward progress and then leaned in to give an illusory embrace. What was up with the guy? It was just a hug, for heaven's sake. She turned back and caught a glimpse of Jennifer. Her eyes twinkled. Quinn thought she saw an almost imperceptible wink before her eyes went over Quinn's right shoulder once again.

"Hello, everyone."

Quinn looked to her right. What was up with the funky hug became clear as she watched a woman pull Ike in for a hug. He returned the embrace. Their eyes met. What was the message she saw in his eyes? An apology perhaps? Who knew? Who cared?

"Hello, Jennifer." Another hug.

"Audrey, always a pleasure."

She turned to Quinn with hand outstretched. "Hi. Audrey Ross."

"Quinn."

"Quinn Taylor, correct?"

"That's me."

"My mom is good friends with your grandmother. Her name is Hillary Ross. Have you met her?"

"No, but I haven't been here long or met many people."

"How long will you be visiting?"

"I've moved here."

"Really?" Quinn noticed Audrey's practiced smile slip a bit. "I would think this town too small for someone like you."

"For the moment, it's just the right size."

Audrey casually slipped her arm through Ike's, causing him to turn from the associate with whom he was speaking. "Yes, Audrey?"

"Did you know that Quinn is not a visitor, but our town's newest resident?"

"Yes, I did."

"Since when do you know PC news before me?" She turned to Quinn. "I must be slacking. But you know, your timing may be favorable. Ike's younger brother is probably around your age and is about to receive his doctorate. Ike, when is Julian coming home?"

"I'm not sure."

"Whenever he arrives, introducing him to this young lady should be at the top of our list."

Ike's gaze went from Audrey to Quinn and back. "Okay."

Quinn understood his rather neutral response. She remembered last night, and the hug, and knew Ike remembered, too. What other answer could he have given?

Audrey's behavior was that of a woman clearly still in love with her ex. Quinn actually felt for her. Ten years was a long time to be in a relationship. How did one go from being in love to being just friends? Quinn knew one way to help the situation was to remove herself from it. Drama was something she didn't need.

"Jennifer, it was good to see you again."

"Good to see you, too, Quinn. Give your grandmother my best."

"I will." She looked briefly at Ike and Audrey. "Bye, guys."

Quinn saw the senior Drake and headed toward him. Her plan was to wish him a happy birthday and make a quiet exit. She wasn't even an employee and now questioned why she'd agreed to come in the first place. She waited until the man with Ike Sr. finished his greeting, but before she could reach him, a woman she'd seen at the office and believed was Ike Sr.'s executive assistant handed him a cordless microphone.

"Good evening, Drake Realty Plus and friends." Chatter began to diminish as those who heard turned toward him. "If I could have everyone's attention, please. Everyone includes you, Terrell."

"Oh, sorry, Dad!" Terrell yelled amid the laughter.

"As long as all that yapping continues to bring us business, I'll cut you some slack. But just a little."

Ike Sr. laughed at his own joke as loudly as everyone else, clearly enjoying himself.

"I just wanted to take a moment and thank you all for coming out to help celebrate my birthday. The older I get, the less I take being another year older for granted. And the more I appreciate all of you, and understand how fortunate I am to work with such a fine group of individuals as those gathered here tonight. That gratitude begins with my family, my sons Ike and Terrell—my son Warren couldn't be here. He wants me to believe he's working—" Ike Sr. used air quotes "—at his vineyard, his ranch. Yeah, likely story, right? He's probably working on opening a bottle of beer.

"All kidding aside, folks…it's probably a can."

More laughter and comments thrown out here and there.

"I'm not sure what I did to deserve it, but even the mayor has graced us with his presence. Mayor Niko Drake, everybody!"

Quinn followed Ike Sr.'s gesture to a handsome, smartly dressed man with an equally attractive woman beside him. As he continued thanking various executives and department heads, Quinn studied the crowd and noted that every Drake mentioned had a woman beside him. Everyone except Ike.

"Last but first is the reason for my breathing."

This comment got Quinn's attention. She refocused on the CEO.

"My lady love, my partner for the last thirty-six years and counting, who I love more today than I did all those years ago, Jennifer Drake. Baby, come up and say something."

Jennifer shook her head.

"Come on, now. People want to see you in that nice outfit. Give her a hand, folks, as she obeys my orders and heads this way."

As expected, Jennifer stopped midstride and gave Ike Sr. a look. The goading and teasing went full force as she laughingly joined her husband. After her brief comments, the party resumed. Quinn hurried forward.

"Mr. Drake?"

He turned. "Yes."

"Hi. I'm Quinn Taylor."

"Good to meet you, Quinn Taylor!" He greeted her enthusiastically while shaking her outstretched hand with one of his big paws, waving at someone else with the other and smiling at an employee who walked by. Five seconds in the presence of this warm, gregarious man and it was clear to Quinn why Drake Realty Plus was a success. "You're the speed demon who jacked my son's car all up, right? Was ordered to our office to work off your punishment."

"Guilty as charged, sir," Quinn said, liking Ike Sr. more as each second passed. "Although I take exception to being called a demon."

"Ha!"

"I was actually an angel, saving a doggy's life."

"Hope that little critter was worth what happened as a result."

"It definitely would have been cheaper to kill him."

Ike Sr. laughed heartily. "You sure are your father's daughter."

"Ike mentioned that you know him."

"Only casually. We've had a battle or two on the golf course, and sat on a committee together several years ago. Haven't seen him lately, though. How's he doing?"

"He's good, sir."

"Next time you talk to him, give him my regards."

"I definitely will. It's been a pleasure speaking with you. I'm leaving but wanted to wish you happy birthday."

"Where are you going? The fun is just beginning."

No, the fun started when Audrey saw me talking to Ike. "I'm going to spend time with my grandmother. Make sure I'm there in case she needs me."

"Well, now. I can't knock that. You take care."

Quinn made a beeline for the door. Ike must have been watching, because before she got halfway to her car, he was calling her name.

"Hey." He caught up with her. "Where are you going?"

"Home." She continued walking toward her car.

He fell into step beside her. "Why?"

"Because I don't want to hang out in a roomful of people I don't know."

"That's fair. What were you and my father discussing?"

"Keeping tabs on me, huh?"

"That probably wouldn't be a bad idea," he muttered.

"I went over to wish him a happy birthday before leaving."

"Oh."

They reached her car. He opened the door. "Be safe. I'll see you tomorrow."

"Goodbye."

He leaned over for a hug. "No, no, no," she half chastised, half teased. "I found out earlier that hugging you publicly is off-limits."

"I wasn't expecting it," he explained. "And I'm not much for PDA."

"Especially when your ex is watching?"

"There was that, too."

"At least you're honest." She looked at him. "Are you going to move so that I can get into my car?"

"After I get a hug?"

She grinned devilishly. "I'll give you a hug, but only if you give me a kiss."

Fully expecting him to deny her, she was shocked when he said, "Okay."

It wasn't a kiss. It was an experience.

He gently touched her lips with his, then rubbed left and right. A delicious friction, something innocent and romantic. Another kiss followed, more pressure this time. His fingers gently massaged the nape of her neck. He stopped.

Looked into her eyes. Lowered his head again. This time, when their lips touched, he swiped across them with his tongue. Hard. Demanding. She'd barely opened her mouth before he plundered it with his tongue. Swirling. Flicking. Sucking her tongue into his mouth. Methodically, meticulously, he kissed her. Quinn felt her core quiver. She placed a hand on his chest, her breathing uneven.

"You okay?"

Not at the moment. Did this man almost just kiss me into a climax? In the parking lot? "I'm fine."

"Be safe."

"You, too."

Quinn relived his kisses the entire way home and knew that nothing in Paradise Cove would ever be the same again.

Chapter 15

"Are the two of you dating? It's none of my business, but you knew I'd ask."

"No, we're not dating."

It was a little after eleven o'clock. Against his better judgment, Ike had given in to Audrey's plea to stop by after leaving the Drake Community Center for coffee and a chat. She'd pointed out that they hadn't seen much of each other lately because of the Ten Drake Plaza deal, which was true. But he also knew that Quinn would be the topic of conversation. He'd agreed, figuring that tonight was as good a time as any to have the discussion and be done with it. Now that it was actually happening, though, he realized he'd much rather be in bed. Or with Quinn. Or both.

"Do you want to date her? It would be easy to see why if you did. She's a beautiful woman."

"Yes, she's gorgeous. No doubt about that."

"But she's so young—what, twenty-two or -three?"

"Twenty-five."

"She doesn't seem like your type. But then again, women like her have a way with anyone possessing a penis."

"What does that mean?"

"No need to jump to her defense. That wasn't meant to be derisive."

"It sounded rather derisive, Audrey."

"I think I need something stronger than coffee." She walked over to her bar. "Care for some liqueur in your cup?"

"No, I'm good. Thanks."

"I watched her interact with your mom and dad. She's

bubbly and flirty, knows what to say to make a man feel good. People period, probably."

"Is that a bad thing?"

Audrey finished mixing her drink and instead of sitting in the chair she'd left, joined Ike on the couch. "No, it's a definite asset. One that has obviously worked on you."

Ike couldn't think of any response to that bomb of a sentence that wouldn't cause it to explode, so he remained quiet.

"No denial?"

"Audrey…"

"No, Ike. Don't feel uncomfortable. I'm not asking this as the jealous ex, but as your friend. That's what we were before we started dating, and that's what we agreed to be now. If you'd rather not discuss her, fine. I'll understand. It's just that I saw how you looked at her when she wasn't watching. Afterward, I tried to remember a time when you looked at me that way. And I couldn't."

"I don't know what you want me to say."

"You don't have to say anything. But as your friend, and someone who still loves you probably more than I should, I want to say this to you. Be careful."

"Audrey, I'm not dating the girl, all right?"

"I know. I hear you. Even so, I still want to say it. I don't have anything against her. I don't know her personally. But I know women like her. And even more, I know you. I know how you love. I don't want to see you hurt. And a woman like her…will crush you."

Ike nodded, finished his coffee and stood.

She did, too. "Now I've run you off. I'm sorry."

"Not at all. If you'll remember, part of my argument in not stopping by was the work I have waiting for me at home." They reached the door. He turned and gave her a light kiss on the forehead.

"I'll always love you, Audrey, and treasure our friendship. But in the future, the details of our love lives—who, what and why we're dating, things like that—are topics that we probably shouldn't discuss."

"Okay."

"You are my friend, and I believe your concern is genuine. But our history of being more than friends makes it uncomfortable to talk about these things with you."

"I understand. I hope you'll be patient with me. For almost ten years you've been the best friend with whom I've shared everything, and I haven't had to censor myself."

"We're still friends. There's just one topic that's off-limits."

"So if I ask whether or not you're going to the masquerade ball, because I was thinking we could go together, you'd say no and not tell me you have a date, or…?"

"What I'd say is…sure, Audrey, we can go together."

"Fantastic." She gave him a hug. "We'll talk later about costumes. Don't work too hard."

On the way out, Ike wrestled with the hurt he'd seen in Audrey's eyes when she mentioned the way he'd looked at Quinn. Even though he didn't have any idea of what look she was talking about, he felt bad. Which was why he'd taken the topic off the table. Yes, they had been best friends. Yes, they had once shared everything. But things were different now. Audrey was a good woman and deserved the marriage and family she craved. Ike's desire was elsewhere and growing stronger with every encounter. As soon as Quinn's internship was over, he'd make his move.

The ringing cell phone startled Ike out of thought. He sighed, knowing how abruptly he'd left Audrey's house. It was probably her. Except the caller ID showed a number he didn't recognize. Who'd be calling this time of night? He let it go to voice mail. When his message indicator dinged, he immediately hit Playback. When the melodic voice came through the speakers, his heart clenched.

"Ike, it's Quinn. I had a quick question and was hoping to catch you. Maybe you're still at the party, or on a booty call. Who knows?" She laughed. "At any rate, give me a call when you can. Thanks."

Ike hit Redial, smiling like a teenage geek who'd just scored the cheerleader. "Hello, Quinn."

"Hey, Ike. That was fast. What, didn't recognize my number and sent me to voice mail?"

"I sent whoever it was to voice mail—couldn't imagine who'd be calling this late."

"You didn't know who, or you didn't know which one. Never mind, don't answer that. It's none of my business."

"You're right. It isn't your business. But the answer at any rate was my initial statement. I didn't know who it was."

"How'd the party turn out?"

"You should have stayed and seen for yourself."

"I wasn't up for an evening of small talk with strangers. I did enjoy meeting your dad, who wasn't present when Grandmother introduced your family. He is such a hoot! Your mom is nice, too, and genuine."

"They're good people."

"I clearly made Audrey uncomfortable. When I left, she probably breathed a sigh of relief."

"I only saw her introduce herself. Was there another conversation?"

"No, only that one, and signs that perhaps only another woman would recognize. Even without a sign, heck, being with someone for ten years can't be something gotten over quickly. And then having to constantly see that person? Definitely a small-town downside."

"Actually, it hasn't been that often. I've practically lived at the office, and when I'm not there I'm usually at home."

"What a boring life, Ike! Dude…we've got to get you a life. Which is why I'm calling, actually."

"To give me a life? I've already got one, thank you, and while it may sound ho-hum to you, it works for me."

"If it works for you, I'm glad you're happy. Does that mean you're going to pass on the masquerade ball?"

"No, I'll be there."

"Great! I'll be there, too."

Not so great, Ike thought, since he'd be there with Audrey.

"You're coming with Mrs. Newman?"

"No, Grandmother isn't planning to attend. I'm bringing my best friend, who'll arrive that weekend. What about you?"

"Audrey asked if I'd escort her. I told her I would."

"Well, don't sound so sad about it, for heaven's sake."

"I'm not sad. Just wondering if agreeing to take her was a good idea."

"Why, because she's still in love with you?"

"I didn't want to think so, but yes. If I'd been thinking clearly, I would have asked you."

"Hmm."

"What does that mean? Can't see yourself out with the boring old guy?"

"That kiss showed me that there's a part of you that isn't boring at all."

"I'd like to show you more. But I'll save that discussion for later. What are you doing on Sunday?"

"I don't know. Why?"

"The birthday celebration will continue with a barbecue at my brother's ranch. I'd love for you to come."

"Is this another company thing?"

"No, more casual, just the family and close friends."

"Including Audrey?"

"No. You'd be my special guest."

"I like feeling special, Mr. Drake. So my answer is yes."

Chapter 16

On Sunday, Quinn arrived at Ike's brother Warren's ranch located in an unincorporated area next to Paradise Cove called Paradise Valley. She was accompanied by her grandmother, who had insisted on driving, since Quinn's license was still restricted. Maggie made it clear that she wouldn't be an accomplice to her granddaughter breaking the law. Almost a dozen cars were parked in the large, paved lot. Maggie eased the trusty sedan she'd been driving for fifteen years into an empty space and cut the motor.

"I know they said not to bring anything," she said, reaching into the back for a container of cookies. "But showing up empty-handed simply isn't polite."

The two women reached a sidewalk that began at the lot and continued around the side of a large, stately home with a wide front porch. They followed the sound of voices until they reached a backyard that seemed to stretch for a mile. Several round tables covered with white tablecloths and decorated with vases of freshly cut flowers were set up on a temporary floor under an open tent in the center of the yard. The day was sunny but crisp. Tall space heaters had been strategically placed among the tables to ward off the chill. Long rectangular tables were on either side of this grouping, loaded with covered trays and dishes. Smaller tables adjacent to one of the longer tables held drinks and desserts. Beyond the table settings and beside a large oak tree were a swing, sandbox and toys where several children played. Adults sat laughing and talking at the tables.

At the same time Quinn saw Ike standing near the play

area with two other men, she spotted Jennifer and another woman coming out of the house. Quinn waved at Jennifer but walked toward Ike. Even with the grass mown so well it resembled carpet, she chose her steps carefully. She'd already made one grand entrance, at the Days of Paradise ball. She didn't want to fall down in her three-inch wedge sandals and be the star attraction again. One of the men Ike was with alerted him of her approaching. He looked up. A slow smile spread across his face, so sexy that even with her concentrated effort to remain upright, her shoe hit a slight dip and she stumbled.

Ike was at her side in an instant. "You okay?"

"I'm fine," she said, looking up just in time to see the men with Ike try and hide their smiles. "Just embarrassed to be your friends' entertainment. And glad I didn't fall."

Ike took her hand, a move that surprised Quinn. Hadn't he said the other night that he wasn't into PDA?

"Quinn, this is my cousin Jackson and my brother Atka. We've decided to drop the in-law part. With us either you're family or you're not. Right, guys?"

Both responded affirmatively and exchanged greetings with Quinn.

"It's nice to meet both of you," Quinn told them. "Now I know you have one sister, at least."

"I have two. Teresa is a twin and married to Atka, and London is the baby of our family."

"Her name is London? I know a model with that name."

Ike looked surprised. "You know my sister?"

Quinn's look mirrored Ike's. "The supermodel who lives in Milan? Always works a bunch of shows for fashion week? That's your sister?"

"Unfortunately."

"Come on now, Ike," Jackson said with a chuckle. "Don't be so hard on her. She hasn't made headlines for the last six months."

"Don't count your chickens," Ike responded.

"I can't believe she's your sister."

"I can't believe you know her. Although now that I think about it, I'm not surprised."

"Why do I get the feeling that that wasn't quite a compliment?"

"Smart woman you've got there, man."

"Absolutely. She graduated Columbia with a dual master's degrees and has been, um, interning at the company."

"Is that how the two of you met?" Atka asked.

"No. She ran into me during the Days of Paradise weekend. Literally."

"This is the woman who smashed your beloved Ferrari? And she gets invited to the family barbecue?" Jackson slowly nodded as he looked at Quinn with understanding. "I'm impressed, Quinn. You must be one heck of a negotiator. What was your major, prelaw?"

"No, my dad is the legal eagle of the family. I have MBAs in business administration and international relations."

"Nice," Atka responded. "Perfect for someone dating this workaholic."

Quinn waited for Ike to correct his brother-in-law. He remained silent, causing Quinn to wonder. *Are we dating now?*

"You're one to talk, Sinclair. Until you met my sister, you lived at the job."

"Pretty much," Atka agreed without hesitation. "Now my job is Teresa."

"I'll tell her you said that," Ike replied as they laughed. "Come on, Quinn. Let's go find his job and I'll introduce you to everybody."

They made the rounds, starting at the table with Ike Sr., Jennifer, Quinn's grandmother and Charli's family, her uncle, Griff, and his lady friend, Alice. Next was Jackson's wife, Diamond, whom Quinn liked right away. She imagined they were about the same age, but Diamond was so put together, effortlessly pretty, refined. Less than five minutes in her presence caused Quinn to ask herself, *What the heck am I going to do with my life?* She was sitting with two other women Ike had introduced.

"You haven't met my brother Niko yet, but this is his wife, Monique."

"Hi, nice to meet you."

"Last but not least—" he motioned toward Teresa "—is Atka's job."

The three women traded confused expressions.

"What does that mean?" Teresa asked.

"Atka made the comment that before getting married, he used to be a workaholic who rarely left work. He said that now you're his job."

Teresa smirked. "Oh, he did, did he?"

Ike asked Quinn, "Did he say that?"

"Yes." Quinn's reply to Ike was directed at Teresa. "And Ike told your husband he'd pass the message along."

"He'd better be glad we have a new guest," Teresa said, getting up from the table and coming their way. "Or I'd give you a message to send back to him that would burn his ears. Hi, Quinn. It's nice to meet you. I apologize in advance for anything you might hear or see—"

The sound of pounding horses' hooves interrupted all conversation. Quinn turned toward the noise. Two expert horsemen raced across a clear and vast expanse of land. Their bodies were in sync with the animals' graceful movements, like a choreographed ballet dancing across the fields. Quinn, who fell in love with horses at boarding school, was in awe.

Just when it appeared that the four-legged friends were going to literally crash the party, a subtle body shift from the riders stopped the horses mere inches from the fence.

"Dammit, Charli! One day I'm going to beat you if it kills me!"

Those who heard chuckled as the rider who'd made the comment dismounted his horse, snatched the well-worn

Stetson from his head and popped Charli on the leg as he passed. If Charli reacted, Quinn couldn't tell. His face was covered with a tan-colored kerchief. He effortlessly swung down from the horse, pulled the kerchief to his neck and took off…her hat?

Quinn was floored. She turned to Ike, gaping. A woman was handling a horse like that?

"Yes," he replied with a nod. "That's how we all felt the first time we saw her ride. Charli!" He waved her over. She strolled past her family, enduring the ribbing and congratulations with the muted reaction her competitor had received.

"Hey, brother," she said when she reached him. Sweat dotted her forehead. She untied the hankie and wiped it. "I'd hug you, but right now you wouldn't appreciate it."

"Probably not," Ike replied. "Looks like you've been riding all over the valley."

"Just down to the fork, around the pond and back. Butterscotch has been restless all day. Had to go wear him out a little." She looked at Quinn. "Hi, I'm Charli."

"And an amazing rider," Quinn said, shaking the outstretched hand. "I'm Quinn. He's a beautiful palomino," she continued, nodding toward the horse now being brushed down by one of the farmhands. "I could tell the two of you have been together for a long time."

"Looks like you got a good one, Ike. Anybody who can spot a fine horse can spot a good man."

Ike's gaze was on Quinn as he responded, "Looks like it. I had no idea."

"Do you ride?" Charli asked.

"Yes. I love horseback riding. Owned a horse named Gaiter years ago, when I lived in Switzerland."

"Would you like to go riding right now?" Charli asked.

"Sure! But…" Quinn looked at her feet.

"You're wearing city duds," Charli said. After giving Quinn a quick once-over, she said, "We can take care of that. Come with me." And over her shoulder as they walked toward the house, she called, "I'll get her ranched up in no time, Ike. You need some jeans, too. Hey, Henry!" A red-haired cowboy looked up. "Saddle up Rosie. I think she'll be a good one for Quinn to ride."

"What about you, Ike?"

"Give me Danger."

"Aw, hell, no!" Warren shouted from the other side of the yard. "You'll not blame me for getting bucked, big brother. You know that horse doesn't ride anyone but me."

Ike came back first. When Quinn and Charli reentered the backyard, conversation all but stopped. Quinn became self-conscious. Why was everyone staring? Quinn had been satisfied with how she looked in the mirror but had told Charli the hat was a bad idea. With two words—*the sun*—she'd insisted.

They gawked because the cosmopolitan chick who'd arrived in three-inch wedges, a black denim pencil skirt and fringed suede jacket had been transformed into a modern-day Annie Oakley. Snug-fitting Levi's, leather cowboy boots and a red-and-blue flannel shirt with a matching hankie, all topped off with a suede and straw cowboy hat.

She looked at Maggie. "Do I look weird as a cowboy, Grandmother?"

Jennifer spoke up. "You look fine, dear. As though you may have roped a steer just this morning."

The group around them laughed. Ike said nothing. Just drank her in like a glass of cold tea in a sultry desert. "We'll be back," he managed as they headed through the fence.

"What do you think, Ike? Could I be the June Carter to your Johnny Cash?"

The question was a brow raiser. "How do you know about them?"

"Um, let's see. How about because they're probably one of the most famous couples in country music?"

"What do you know about country music?"

"Ike Drake, you have no idea what I know."

They reached the barn and walked inside. "I'm ready to see how well you can sit a horse."

"Those two right there, Mr. Drake. All saddled up and ready to ride."

"Thanks, Henry."

Henry stopped in front of Quinn, reached into the stained suede jacket that hid a paunch belly and pulled out an apple. "Rosie loves these and likes her nose rubbed, too. You won't have to shout at her, and you don't want to. It might spook her. We got her when she was two years old and think something bad happened with noises when she was a colt."

Quinn took the apple. "Thanks, Henry."

Looking directly into Rosie's eyes, Quinn slowly approached the stall. "Hello, Miss Rosie," she said, her voice soft and friendly. "You're a pretty horse. You're really pretty."

She stopped in front of the stall and rubbed Rosie's nose. She could tell that the horse was intrigued but a little nervous.

"I know you don't know me, but there's no need to be scared. I love horses. My name is Quinn. Would you like an apple?"

She lifted it to the horse's mouth. Rosie thanked her by using her teeth to pick it up and wolfing it down in two bites.

Quinn laughed. "Good girl." She rubbed the horse's nose and continued talking to her as she entered the stall, placed a foot in the stirrup and easily swung herself up on the saddle.

"I'm impressed," Ike said. After he mounted a majestic-looking black mustang, the two set out across the plains, settling into a comfortable trot for the first part of the ride.

Quinn raised her head to the sun. This experience took her back to when she was sixteen years old. She used to spend all day outside, playing sports and riding Gaiter. Only now did she realize just how much she missed it.

"What's going on in that beautiful head of yours?"

"So that's your question? Earlier, when I asked how I looked, you didn't answer."

"That's because I was in shock, wondering how someone in jeans and flannel could still look so fine."

The comment made Quinn feel all girly and warm. "Thank you."

"I haven't done this in a while. Forgot how relaxing and therapeutic it could be."

"That's what I was thinking."

"About your horse? What was his name?"

"Gaiter."

"I would never have guessed you'd know about horses or anything to do with land and nature."

"That's because you just met me. I used to be a tomboy—" Quinn glanced at Ike "—and a bit of a geek."

He made a sound of disbelief. "I doubt that."

"It's true. Remember, I was raised by a man and grew up knowing more about football stats and the stock exchange than I did about the latest fashion. While Grandmother made sure I was well-rounded with lessons in violin and ballet, Dad and I were more likely to spend the weekends on the golf course, riding bikes or playing some type of ball. I played sports in high school."

"Which ones?"

"Soccer and track. And I rode Gaiter, a lot."

"What happened to that girl and when did the woman I met come along?"

"Just before I turned seventeen, when I met my best friend, Trent."

"A dude helped you become a woman?"

Quinn laughed. "No, but he probably could. He used to model—which is how I met London, by the way—and was super conscious about appearance. Not to the point of being conceited, although many may have seen it that way, but more because of how he wanted to be viewed in the world. Anyway, he invited me to a really upscale party. It was after some awards show, I don't remember which one. But what I do remember is his expression when he came to get me and saw what I had on."

She laughed at the memory.

"That bad, huh? What were you wearing?"

"Something I thought made me look super hot! It was a floral-print dress with these two-inch granny-like navy heels. I was a mess!" Her laughter turned into an all-out guffaw. "What was I thinking?" she yelled, as if the sky had answers.

And off she went. First Rosie, bolting forward at the loud noise. Then Quinn, falling backward off the horse. "Ow!"

Ike jumped down and rushed over to where Quinn lay in a heap. He dropped to his knees.

"Are you okay?"

Quinn moaned as she tried to sit up.

"No, wait. Don't move yet. Let me see if anything's broken."

He placed a hand beneath her knee, and with gentle squeezes examined her leg from ankle to thigh.

"Where does it hurt?"

"My head. I think I hit a rock or something."

He carefully raised Quinn's head and felt beneath it. There was a rock. Not that big, about the size of a golf ball, but with an ugly ridge that, hit just right, could do damage. He turned her head to the side, threaded his fingers through her hair to her scalp, and used his fingertips to check for bruises.

Ike did this because he was a kind, compassionate man genuinely concerned about her health. Had he been a doctor, he might have known that the scalp was an erogenous zone covered with nerves extremely sensitive to the touch. Or considered that massaging her scalp released serotonin and oxytocin, feel-good hormones. It might have crossed his mind that the brain was the body's biggest sex organ.

But Ike wasn't a doctor, and he had no idea how much he was turning Quinn on.

Rearing back so he could see her face, he delivered his report. "You might end up with a bump, but there's no bleeding. I think you'll live."

"Me, too," Quinn lazily responded as she reached a hand behind Ike's neck and pulled his face forward.

He didn't resist but was taken aback. "What are you doing?"

Quinn didn't answer, figuring he'd know soon enough.

His lips were as soft and cushiony as she remembered. She brushed hers back and forth across them, as he'd done before, swiped her tongue along his lips' seam. They parted. He moaned, as if his tongue had accepted the invitation to tangle without its owner's consent. He was hot and wet, the subtle scents of his cologne—bergamot, cedarwood, saffron, sage—wrapped around her like a hug. *Good idea.* She lifted her other arm and pulled Ike's body on top of hers. The warmth of his body chased away the autumn chill. The goose bumps stayed, though, brought on by the slow and thorough way Ike plundered her mouth, her nipples pebbling against his hard chest.

The kiss deepened, their bodies shifted. Soon Ike's hand had slid from her neck to her denims. He squeezed her soft cheeks. His manhood hardened. Quinn shivered as she felt the bulge grow. She swirled her hips beneath him, encouraging, welcoming. Her fingers raked his back. She wanted him now, here, in the middle of the field. She didn't care who might see them.

Ike did. He sat up abruptly, then staggered to his feet. His breath came in quick, short spurts. The front of his pants resembled a bronzed codpiece. She sat up, the fall all but forgotten, and began to stand. Two steps and he was there, helping her up.

"What was that?" he asked, still shaken.

Using her fingers, Quinn swept her hair into a ponytail,

then retrieved the hat on the ground and put it on. Then she stepped toward him, defiantly. "A kiss. Ike Drake style. Because I like how you do it. And I might do it again."

His deep brown eyes seared into her. He took a step as well. Quinn held her ground. Men like Ike probably resented women who took the lead. Too bad. There was no way she'd apologize for a kiss as good as that.

The attraction was like an electrical charge crackling between them. Ike's eyes sank down to Quinn's lips, then he asked her, "What are you waiting for?"

The second kiss was better than the first.

"We'd better stop now," he said once he released her. "While we still can. Plus, dinner's probably ready. We should get back."

Quinn shielded her eyes and looked around her. "I wonder where Rosie went."

"Probably home. Come on. We'll ride together."

As they mounted his horse and headed back to the ranch, Quinn couldn't stop thinking about how many ways she wanted to ride this man.

Chapter 17

He needed all the sleep he could get. Yet an hour after showering and crawling into his custom-made California king bed, Ike was wide-awake. Thinking about Quinn. Having someone occupy almost every free moment he had to think was a new experience. Something about her had caused Ike to look differently at every area of his life.

He punched and repositioned the pillow. Maybe the sleep evading him while on his left side would find him on his right. Quinn, the social butterfly turned country cowgirl. That startling transformation had blown his mind. She was a perfect fit into his family. It took a special kind of person to navigate the Drakes. Quinn had done so effortlessly. In less than fifteen minutes, she'd won over everyone at the ranch. She'd even gotten Warren's neighbor Griff to laugh out loud, something Warren said hadn't happened since cars had eight-track tapes.

Then there was Quinn, the horseback rider. Seeing her with her jeans-clad round booty astride Rosie, feet clad in a pair of Charli's cowboy boots, hair stuffed under a cowboy hat that had never looked so sexy, stirred a part of his soul that hadn't been touched since summers on his grandpa's farm. Back then he'd envisioned a life like his grandfather's—a large farm with acres of land, lots of animals and a fully stocked pond. A wife like his grandmother, who could sew a suit in the morning, catch a bucket of fish in the afternoon and then cook them up for dinner along with biscuits and gravy and peach cobbler from scratch.

All while being a lady, her hair always coiffed, her voice kind and gentle.

That all changed when he turned sixteen. That summer, instead of going to the farm, he accepted an invitation to attend a two-week symposium for college-bound students with a high aptitude for business. Ike had originally declined the offer. Everything he wanted to know about business was as close as a chat with his dad. Ike Sr. had expressed his desire for Ike to join the company but had also encouraged him to follow his heart, which was on the farm with his grandpa. He'd told his math teacher as much when he declined the offer.

But Mr. Anderson was an excellent teacher who knew how to motivate. He told Ike that not attending was probably best. That the workshops would be strenuous and even though the symposium was only for the best students across the country, and Ike was the smartest guy in his small-town class, this level of learning would probably be too much for him. When Ike left the classroom, the application for the conference was in his book bag. His love of land and knack for numbers were gently guided into the decision that led to an MS in business with an emphasis in real estate and sustainability. That Quinn also had a master's in business had totally surprised him. That she loved horses and could sit one well was unexpected, too. He imagined she was full of surprises. And was even more alarmed that he wanted to know them all.

Frustrated that the sleep he chased stayed one step ahead of him, Ike threw back the covers and got out of bed. Halfway to the door and the nighttime tea he remembered was in his cupboard, the phone rang.

The clock on the nightstand read twelve forty-five. Fearing a family emergency, he picked up the phone without checking the ID.

"Ike Drake." No response. Ike was already frustrated

from not being asleep. Bad timing for a prank phone call. He spoke again, more brusquely, demanding. "Hello?"

"Um, Ike, it's me, Quinn." Her voice was soft, a bit unsteady.

Her voice sent shock waves through very specific parts of his body. "Quinn, what's going on? You sound frightened."

"You sound angry. I probably woke you up."

"Not at all." Ike stepped into house slippers and headed downstairs. "In fact, I'm headed downstairs right now for a cup of sleepy tea."

"What's that, tea with bourbon in it?"

"No, but that might not be a bad idea, either. It's an herbal concoction. I have no idea what kind of herbs or whether it will work. But after tossing and turning for over an hour, I'm willing to give it a try."

"Having a problem sleeping, huh?"

"Yep."

"Me, too."

"Is that why you're calling?"

Only a slight hesitation before the reply. "That's part of the reason."

"What's the other part?" Teapot filled and on the stove, Ike pulled the herbal tea and a mug from one cabinet and packets of raw sugar from the other. He walked over to the fridge, opened it, won the battle to not have a late-night snack and closed the door. "Quinn. What's the other part?"

He heard an exasperated sigh before words spilled out rapidly, one after another. "The other part is that I've been here for three months with no sex and no prospects. That kiss set my body on fire and you've got the hose that can put it out!"

The barrage was unexpected. Her explanation direct. Ike vacillated between incredulity and a begrudging respect. Honesty ranked high among virtues Ike valued.

"I guess you weren't expecting that."

Ike chuckled. "Not at all."

"Well, what's the answer?"

"Absolutely not."

She sighed. "I knew you'd say that."

"If you knew, why'd you ask?" Ike poured hot water over the tea bags he'd placed in the cup, put a lid over the brew and walked back upstairs.

"Because I couldn't stop thinking about your fire hose and was pretty sure it could, you know, put out all of my flames. But then I said to myself, *He's old-fashioned and will probably think I'm being too aggressive*."

"You don't think that was an aggressive question?"

"Not at all. You asked me why I called. I told you."

"Because you're looking for fire hoses."

"Because I'm looking for your fire hose. The one pressed against my thigh this afternoon in the grass, and when I shifted, it was hot and hard against my—"

"Quinn!"

"Yes, Ike?"

The question asked with a sultry feigned innocence only served to increase Ike's discomfort. He reached his bedroom, but lying down? Not in this condition. Going to sleep? Highly unlikely. His body hummed. His penis throbbed. He needed to end this call or else he'd explode.

"I'm going to hang up now."

"I knew you were a jerk."

"Ha! I'm a jerk now? Again?"

"Yes," she said with a pout.

"How do you figure?"

"Because if you were a nice guy you'd help me. Don't I sound like a damsel in distress?"

"You sound like the spoiled woman I met in the town square."

"Let's have sex, Ike."

"Good night, Quinn."

"You know you want to." Her voice dropped, became breathy, raspy. "I've never been with someone like you. An older man, handsome, experienced, with that broad chest I can still feel crushing my breasts. And the way you kiss. You want to know my favorite thing about you so far?"

He told himself not to respond, that he didn't want or need to hear the answer. "What?"

"Your tongue. It felt so amazing in my mouth, I can only imagine how it would feel licking me all over, everywhere."

"I'm hanging up."

"Okay, Mr. Drake. But when you see me later at the ball? Know that what's on my mind now will be on my mind then. Good night."

Ike tossed the phone on the bed and headed straight for the shower, took one as cold as he could stand. That helped to deflate the hose, but sleep was still a long time coming. Why hadn't he taken Quinn up on her offer? It's what he wanted, what he'd told himself he'd go after as soon as she left the company. Even as he asked these questions, though, he knew the answer. Fear. Plain and simple. Quinn's unpredictable, spontaneous, free-spirited nature didn't work in the safe, ordered life Ike had created and until now enjoyed. He liked being in control. Of everything. He rarely went into a situation until he was sure that the outcome would be in his favor. Ike recalled Audrey's warning—*A woman like that will crush you.*

Perhaps, Ike mused, as his eyelids finally began to droop. *But it's a risk I'll have to take.* Because the same thing that Quinn said would be on her mind was now on his mind, too.

Chapter 18

Quinn ran down the stairs and out the door. "Trent!"

A tall, slender man jumped out of the car, wrapped his arms around Quinn's waist and twirled her around. "Q-Tip! What's up, girl!" He eased her down and away from him as he held her hands. "I thought these months in the country would drive you insane, but look at you! Still couture!"

"You're such a nut. I missed you!" They hugged again. "Come on, let's grab your stuff and go inside. Are you tired? Have you eaten?"

"I'm exhausted and starved. But the trip was worth it. He got the house. Did I tell you?"

"No. Did he get a good deal?"

"An amazing deal, considering there's so few properties available and his is near the beach. The house needs a lot of work, but once that happens the value will soar."

"I'm glad it worked out for your uncle. And I'm so excited to see you!"

They entered Maggie's immaculately restored bungalow. "We'll take your luggage upstairs," Quinn said, reaching for his hand. "Then we'll go for grub and gossip. I want to hear about the latest goings on in Paris and what you did back east."

"Whoa, wait. Where's Mrs. Grandma?"

"She's having lunch with a friend. Now, come on!"

"I've waited so long to meet her," Trent complained as they thumped up the stairs.

"She's preparing a special dinner tomorrow…just for you."

Thirty minutes later Quinn and Trent arrived at Acquired Taste and took the booth farthest from the front door and bar. With her motley crew of friends, Quinn was sure there'd be stories meant for her ears alone. Both were starving, so they placed their food and drink orders at the same time. The waiter hadn't taken two steps from the table before the gossip began.

"Guess who's dating Max Tata. It's the first text I saw after landing in Sacramento."

"I don't know who that is. What do I care?"

"Oh, Lord. You really are out of touch. Do they even have internet in this town? Or cable?"

"Oh, shut up."

"Max is only the biggest producer/director in Hollywood right now. Or the world, for that matter. He produces the fanatica films."

"Huh?"

"They're a cross between fantasy and erotica, soft porn meets suspense-filled fantasy. Lots of smoke and mirror–type filming. Is she naked? Did they really just show her lady bits?"

"Ha!"

"Stuff like that. They're hard to explain, but the femme fatale leads of the first two movies are now poised to become A-list stars. He's said to have the Midas touch, the ability to turn an unknown into an international star with just one movie. Oh, and he also tends to have them in his bed throughout the process. Does the name Shelly Madden ring a bell?"

"Of course! She's in that controversial underwear ad and has been on TMZ a few times. Who doesn't know her?"

"Her star power was created by Max Tata. Before starring in his film she was waiting tables at a café in Bulgaria, her native country!"

"Wow." Quinn reached for her phone and went online.

"They just went through a really nasty breakup. She

didn't want to leave the lap of luxury and all the perks that come with simply being with a guy like him. She complained of not knowing many people in America and having nowhere to live. So get this, he bought her a house, spent a half a frickin' million dollars just to get her out of his—ten-million-dollar mansion in Pacific Palisades, but I digress—and she still refused to leave. That was the breaking news about a month or so ago, while you were obviously under a rock."

"I was doing time at Drake Realty Plus," Quinn replied, her eyes glued to internet pics of Shelly as she scrolled her phone.

"The police were called and there was a three-hour standoff before they got tired of the nonsense and bum-rushed her ass!

"But this just in, hot off the private Trent Corrigan press." His hushed voice exhibited the excitement he felt. "Just two days ago, he showed up at a private dinner, no cameras allowed, with the new girl. Telling folks all about how she was the star in his next movie, one that would be bigger than the first two combined."

"So…who is it?"

"Guess."

"Really, Trent? After that soliloquy of a buildup you're still holding out?"

"Okay, okay. It's London."

"The model London?"

"No, the bridge. Of course the model, silly. Who else do we both know with that name?"

"And this next film is going to be like the others, with erotica and stuff."

"From what I hear, it's going to be the sexiest one yet, really pushing the R-rated envelope. But you can't say anything about this. To anyone. I'm not even supposed to know.

"On the way here, I called her but got voice mail. I wasn't surprised. At least it was still her number. For now. Our girl London, a movie star. Isn't that wild? Imagine what this means for our social calendar! But mum's the word, promise?"

"We share everything in confidence," Quinn said sincerely. "You know that."

Two years older and worlds wiser, beautiful bi Trent was the one who'd introduced Quinn into the circle of young, beautiful, wealthy expats to which London belonged. He'd met London when he was dating a designer who booked her for a number of runway shows. They'd partied together and whenever she was in Paris they'd hang out.

The waiter delivered their drinks.

Quinn pulled her glass closer. "I can't believe it. London, an actor? Who knew?"

"Nobody, apparently. But that doesn't necessarily matter to a good director. The perfect woman, the right shot and fifty takes if necessary to get the desired scene and voilà! Anyone can be amazing."

He lifted his glass. "Here's to movies and mayhem in Paradise Cove."

"Calm down, Trent. *Mayhem* is a strong word. You're just visiting. I have to live here."

She said it to try to lighten the mood but secretly thought he'd delivered a prophecy.

"Are you getting soft on me? Since when do you care what people think?"

Since meeting Ike.

"Do you think I'm serious? You actually look…I don't know…worried."

Troubled was a better word. The odds had to be a billion to one that so many coincidences would collide into one big ball of *WTH?* Meeting London in Europe and then running into her brother, literally, on the other side of the ocean. Receiving the weirdest form of community service ever, working with London's brother, toward whom she then developed a crazy attraction, and then learning the family might be doing business with a potentially deadly international gang of political and business thugs. But was this enough? Oh, no! Why not throw a soon-to-be porn star into the mix? One who happened to be the mayor's sister and a member of one of the town's founding families. And by the way, she had to keep her mouth shut about it all. Since she'd talked to Ike about the report, she'd all but forgotten about it and its implications. This latest news placed it back in the now crowded spotlight of secrets. And put her in the middle of the mayhem Trent foretold.

He placed a hand on her arm. "Hey, you okay?"

"Oh, yeah, I'm fine."

"You sure?"

"Yeah, I'm sorry for spacing out like that."

"I wouldn't have told you if I'd known you'd get upset."

"No, I mean, what you just shared is definitely a lot to take in. But a thought popped into my head about something at work, and I got distracted."

"Hey! Tell me about that. What does it feel like to work a nine to five?"

Quinn had never been so happy to talk about Drake Realty Plus in all of her life. "I thought it would suck, but it wasn't so bad."

"You used the past tense. Are your thirty days over?"

"Yes, but Lydia, the woman who trained me, was swamped last week. Then her kid got sick on Friday and she had to leave early. So she asked me to come in a couple days next week just to make sure everything I'd been given was either completed or transferred to someone else. And since this is post-penalty, I'll earn my first paycheck!"

"You say that as though it's a good thing."

"Excuse me. I forgot I was talking to a trust-fund child who'll likely not work a day in his life."

"That's not true. I just won't work a conventional job. But don't get upset. If you're happy, I'm thrilled. But enough corporate talk. Reminds me of my father, who's like your father, pushing us in directions we don't want to go. I'm about to break out in hives. Let's have another drink. Waiter!"

"Oh, I almost forgot." Quinn reached again for her phone, pulled up a picture and turned the screen toward Trent.

"Adam and Eve." He looked at Quinn, a brow raised. "Is this a clue about something?" She nodded. "You've taken up gardening."

"Hardly."

"You went to church with your grandmother."

"Not yet, but she's pushing."

"You...made an apple pie?"

Quinn cracked up. "It us, you nut. These are the costumes I ordered for tonight's masquerade ball."

Trent snatched the phone. "I don't know, Quinn. I'm not sure Adam's loin leaf is big enough for me, know what I'm sayin'?"

"I know what you're implying. Sounds like a page from one of Tata's fantasy films."

"Ha! This is a pretty cool idea. I like it." He smiled at her, eyes gleaming. "From the woman who balked when I mentioned mayhem."

"What?" She reached for the phone and studied the pic. "They're a tad racy, but everything's covered. There were options that exposed way more skin than this. One had the guy wearing just a big leafed G-string and the woman touting pasties with a leafy thong."

"That's the one you should have ordered!"

"I wanted to," Quinn admitted. "But as I said before, I live here."

After leaving the restaurant, Quinn directed Trent around parts of Paradise Cove on the east side, where Quinn lived. When they returned home, her grandmother was there to greet them with freshly baked chocolate chip cookies. Trent fell in love on the spot. For the next couple hours Trent took a nap and Quinn went to her spa treatment. When she returned, they got ready and headed to the ball.

It had started at eight, but Quinn waited until almost nine to make her entrance. At first she'd been unsure about the costume she'd ordered, but when her grandmother saw it and didn't pass out, her confidence was restored.

"Ready, Adam?"

"Absolutely, Eve."

"Good. Let's start tongues a-wagging."

From the time Ike entered the ballroom, he was distracted. Waiting. Wondering. Looking toward the door. Anticipating her arrival. He remembered how she looked at the other ball, during the Days of Paradise weekend. The dress with a back so low it showed the crack of dawn. Too much skin showing, making him want her. Along with every other man in the room. With that as her outfit for a regular dance, he couldn't begin to imagine how she'd be dressed tonight.

"Look at you, two! How adorable!"

A woman dressed in 19th-century Victorian style, complete with a hoopskirt and tightly laced corset, floated toward them. One hand clasped her gold mask's stick, the other a glass of champagne. From the shrill sound of her voice, it wasn't her first.

Ike easily recognized Audrey's coworker. But in the spirit of the evening, he adopted a cool stance and adjusted his sunglasses. "Who are you?"

"Why, kind sir. My name be Victoria, Queen of London." She executed a curtsy and promptly stumbled. The champagne splashed in Ike's direction. He jumped back but some of it still hit the side of his suit coat.

"Oh, no, Ike. I'm so sorry."

"I'm not Ike. I'm Jay."

Audrey lowered her voice. "And I'm Kay."

"And we," they said together, "are the men in black."

Victoria didn't seem too impressed. Ike didn't care. He wasn't big on masquerades, Halloween or costumes, but had come out to be supportive. When Audrey suggested dressing as the characters in one of his favorite movies, he was all in. Black suit, sunglasses, oversize gun and boom. Ready for the masquerade.

"Excuse me, ladies. I'm going to get something to wipe off my suit."

The bathrooms were near the front entrance. He'd just come out when the room began to buzz. He saw heads turning, necks craning, people talking behind their hands. Without a glimpse or a doubt he knew what had happened—Quinn had entered the building. He braced himself for something outrageous and stepped beyond the plant that blocked his view. The sight of her took his breath.

Eve. *Of course. I should have known.* She stood tall and elegant in a flesh-colored catsuit. Only a spattering of strategically placed leaves stood between her and a public nudity charge. She wore a wig that reached her waist, a simple red mask and bright red lipstick. A sparkly evening purse shaped like an apple dangled from a delicate wrist. Ike wasn't much of a religious man, but he'd heard the creation story and felt sorry for Adam. Because if Ike had faced a woman who looked like Quinn just now, he, too, would have eaten the apple. Heck, who was he fooling? He would have eaten the whole darn tree!

She spotted him, said something to the couple and the guy beside her, and headed his way.

Keep cool, Ike. She's only a woman. He was thankful for the glasses that hid the lust in his eyes. As long as his heart didn't beat out of his chest…he'd be fine.

"The man in black," she cooed as she sidled up to him. "Which one are you? Jay or Kay?"

His face and voice were void of expression. "Isn't it obvious?"

"Probably but I don't remember. Trent—I mean, Adam—which one was the black guy?"

"I think Jay."

"Hello, Jay."

"Hello."

"I'd like you to meet my best friend, Trent, tonight known as Adam."

Ike barely turned his head. "Hello, Adam."

"Adam, in another world Jay's name is Ike."

"How ya doin', man?" They shook hands. "He's pretty good!" Trent laughed as he talked to Quinn. "Has the whole cold stare down, the attitude, everything! Hey, I'm going to get a drink. What do you want?"

"Just sparkling water for now. Thanks."

Neither Ike nor Quinn watched Trent leave. They only had eyes for each other.

"I'm surprised your grandmother let you out of the house."

"She did, and with her blessings. Said my costume perfectly captured Eve in the garden. The only thing I'm missing—" she took a step closer, ran a fingernail across the back of his hand "—is your snake."

With that, she turned and melted into the crowd, leaving him and his snake pulsing.

He took it as long as he could. For thirty whole minutes, a record, considering he hadn't thought he'd make it for five. Then he excused himself from Audrey for a final time and went to find her. It wasn't hard. She and "Adam" were dancing on the ballroom floor.

"Excuse me, Adam," Ike said, adopting the authoritative tone of the character he portrayed. "I'm conducting an investigation and need to speak to the witness."

Without another word, he grabbed Quinn's hand and led them to the door.

Chapter 19

Ike's heart pounded. His heat-seeking missile throbbed even harder. He was acting totally unlike himself and didn't give a damn. Right now all he wanted was him, Quinn, together, alone. It had been a mistake to deny her, to dismiss the need she'd so clearly and passionately articulated last night.

"Ike! Slow down. Where are we going?"

"My house. Sorry, I forgot about your heels."

"Wait! I'm not leaving."

Ike stopped abruptly and turned around. "We're going to my house," he began, his voice low and urgent as he leaned close to her face, "where I am going to make long, slow, delicious love to you all night long. I am sorry that this didn't happen last night. But the closest I can get to changing the past…is to give you the present." Without warning he pulled her into him, placed his hands on her butt and pressed his rock hardness into her soft flesh. He watched her eyes widen and then flutter closed. "I really want to give it to you," he whispered, tracing her ear with his tongue as he took another slow turn of his hips.

"Ike…"

"I want to make up for not being spontaneous, adventurous, exciting."

"I appreciate that, but you know I didn't come here alone."

"Send him a text."

"We were on the dance floor. My purse is inside!"

Ike let out a frustrated groan. "You're driving me crazy."

"I know how that feels."

"Then help me…help you."

The line was lame but delivered with such emotion they laughed anyway.

"Ike, it would be rude to leave Trent."

"Didn't I see him talking to someone?"

"Yes, my friend Peyton. But they just met."

"He's a grown man. And you're a grown woman. Tell him you have something grown to handle." To bring the point home, he reached for her hand and placed it on his burgeoning snake.

Quinn wasn't shy. She examined the length and breadth of his package like a postal inspector. "I'll be right back."

"I'll get the car."

By the time Ike had retrieved the car and pulled it around to the building's entrance, his erection had diminished as his conscience increased. Had he really just pulled a half-naked woman off the dance floor, out of the club and into the fall chill? With the attraction that Quinn was in Paradise Cove, his actions had certainly not gone unnoticed. And what about Audrey? Was he to follow his own advice? Tell her he had to handle some grown folks' business and to hitch a ride with Queen Victoria?

He ran a frustrated hand across a bewildered brow. This wasn't him. A tempestuous, impetuous imbecile who abandoned dates. An undisciplined dunce who showed out in public. His had always had a healthy sexual appetite, but nothing as raw and animalistic as what led to him channeling Tarzan and dragging Jane into the cold.

"I can't do this." He scrolled his contacts for Quinn's number and had just tapped the phone icon as she walked out the door. He ended the call. The doorman rushed to open the car door and help her inside.

"Okay, all set," she announced, her eyes bright and shiny.

"We can't do this."

"I agree. Having sex in this driveway would be totally

obtuse. Which is why you need to step on it and get to Golden Gates pronto. Break the law if you have to, but get us there quick. You've got me so turned on!"

She reached for him. He stayed her hand. "Quinn, stop."

"Look, Trent's fine. I left him in Peyton's most capable and willing hands. I wouldn't doubt if they throw a party like we're about to before the night is over."

"I forgot all about Audrey. If I leave without her, she'll be very upset."

"Who was just telling me about being grown? Never mind. I forgot who I'm dealing with."

Quinn reached for the door. Ike reached for Quinn. "Wait."

Once again, he tapped the phone icon on the steering wheel and turned up the volume.

Audrey's voice shot out like an accusatory arrow. "Ike? Where are you?"

"I'm outside, Audrey. In the car."

"What? Why didn't you say we were leaving? I've been looking all over for you. Give me a minute to get my—"

"Audrey." His tone was more forceful than intended, spurred by guilt and resolve. "Don't worry about leaving the party. I'll arrange a car to be waiting for when you're ready to go home."

A long pause. "Does this have anything to do with why I don't see Quinn Taylor? Are you being tempted, and if so...will you fall?"

Ike thought about reminding her that this topic was off-limits. But given the situation, she had a right to know.

"Quinn is with me, Audrey. I feel bad, and I'm so sorry to hurt—"

Audrey hung up.

Ike's shoulders slumped.

"It's okay," Quinn said, her eyes filled with empathy. "We can go back inside."

"No." Ike put the car in gear and eased away from the curb. "I'm where I want to be."

The drive from the Paradise Cove Country Club to Ike's home in Golden Gates was quiet and, thankfully, brief. It was a comfortable silence, thrumming with sexual tension wrapped in anticipation. Soft sounds of smooth jazz complemented the vibe. Ike reached for Quinn's hand and squeezed it. She squeezed back.

They reached his home. He pulled into the garage and cut the engine.

"Just about everything about me has been different since you happened."

"Since I happened?"

He slid eyes shielded by lowered lids in her direction. "Yes. At first, I described that incident as an accident that happened. Later I came to realize that what happened to me…is you."

"I hope you don't expect me to pay for any damages that can't be verified with a legitimate estimate and receipt. A 1961 Ferrari was the only item of restitution included in the judge's order."

"We don't have to worry about that. Any pain from now on will be the good kind."

He leaned over, brushed her lips with his and exited the car. Once he'd unlocked the door, he stepped aside so she could enter his home. That's where foreplay started. Right there. At the door.

He turned her around, pressed her against it with his body, her fur coat unfastened, her scantily clad body absorbing his heat. His lips touched hers, just barely. Once, then again. His tongue took the same journey along the crease of her lips, swiping across until she opened up, and then delving inside her mouth in search of its twin. He kissed her lovingly, hungrily, thoroughly, as though she were the rays to his sunshine, the wetness of his rain. With an intensity that suggested in this moment one could not happen without the other. As though she was as necessary as oxygen and more crucial to his existence than the arteries that pumped blood to his heart.

The kiss ended. Ike touched his forehead to hers and took deep breaths to calm down. "You drive me crazy," he admitted. "I'm going to have to slow down and take my time with you. Let's get comfortable."

They reached the coat closet. Ike stepped behind Quinn and removed her floor-length faux fur. He slid it off her shoulders, down her arms and released it to the floor. Wrapping his arms around her from behind, he squeezed her tightly and inhaled her scent. Let his fingers travel from her waist to the hardened nipples standing out against the leaves that covered them. With a firm grip on each petal, he yanked hard. The flimsy material ripped. Her weighty globes jiggled in the unexpected freedom.

"Oh! There is a zipper, you know," Quinn managed between halting breaths as Ike came around and sucked a firm bud into his mouth. He swirled his tongue around the areola as his hand reached down and cupped her flower, touched the moisture his kiss had created. He stood upright, looked into her eyes as he grasped the leaf covering the paradise he would soon enter and tore it off.

"Don't say a word," he commanded before Quinn could speak. "I've let you have your way long enough. Tonight, I'm in control."

He eased her down, right there, to the faux fur's silky lining. She lay back as he placed a hand on each knee and pushed her legs apart. Feathery kisses began just below her knee and moved up to her thigh—alternating from one leg to the other. And to the inner thigh, his tongue hot and wet, lapping the exposed skin, creating a friction with the mesh that raised goose bumps on Quinn's bared skin. To the juncture of her thigh, nibbling an area just beneath the pelvic bone, close to but not quite touching the quivering bud within her flower. Over and again, he bit and licked while his fingers played a massaging melody up and down her thighs.

"Ike! Please..."

He threw off his coat. Grabbed the fabric on both sides of the torn area below and pulled. The material ripped up the middle, leaving Quinn exposed. Wet. Ready. He bent down, his mouth hovering just above the spot. He stuck out his tongue for a tiny taste, flicked it back and forth. Quinn writhed, lifted her hips off the floor, offered herself freely, completely. She tried to direct him, take over, speed things up. But Ike wasn't having it. He stayed there. Flicking. Licking. Blowing on the wetness. Gently sucking and tugging on her petals, as if hers was the rarest of blooms.

Sitting back on his haunches, he stared at her. She raised her knees to bring her legs together.

"No. I want to see you. I want to imprint the image of your desire on my tongue and in my mind."

He gazed, and suddenly there was no more room in the crotch of his slacks. He stood then, continued to stare at her as he removed his cuff links, tie and shirt. Unfastened his belt, released the zipper and stepped out of his slacks. Adjusting his erection inside the roomy boxers, he knelt down and kissed her navel, ran his lips across the smooth bikini wax to the clean-shaven lips. Once there he slowly lowered his face to them and engaged in a French kiss of the feminine flower that lasted ten minutes. Quinn's climax was an out-of-body experience.

Turned out, Ike was just getting started.

He picked her up, carried her up a wrought-iron staircase that in itself was a work of art. His hooded eyes never left hers as he reached for a condom and slid it over his long, thick dick. He took his time. Tapping the entrance to her paradise, going deeper each time, until he finally raised his hips and plunged himself fully inside her. Set up a slow, easy rhythm. Easing out. Thrusting in. He ground his hips in a slow, circular motion. Quinn matched the movement, her hips swirling and pulsing to the beat. Slow. Easy. Hard. Deep. He raised her legs and shifted.

"Ah!"

And hit that spot.

Once.

Twice.

A third time.

Then finally, when he was sure he'd given Quinn all she could handle and more, he pumped himself to paradise, too.

Chapter 20

Quinn prepared to turn over and hit a wall. She scrunched her eyes, momentarily confused. How could that happen? Her bed was in the middle of the room. She shifted her legs, felt the sweet soreness between her thighs and remembered everything. She turned from her side to her back and stared at the intricate designs on the gilded tray ceiling. A contented sigh escaped her lips.

Ike heard, squeezed her shoulder, ran his hand down her arm and rested it on her bare thigh. She repositioned her pillow and snuggled back against him. Last night, all night, had been the surprise of her life. Not only was his direct, tenacious behavior totally out of character, but the intensity of his lovemaking was beyond anything she could have dreamed. The geeky old man in khakis and a polo, the unfeeling jerk with a cold heart. Definitely him on that day when they met in the town square. But last night, when he'd carried her to bed after sexing her senseless from the garage to the second-floor stairs, it was like meeting him again for the very first time. And if what she was beginning to feel against her booty cheeks was any indication, the meeting was about to continue.

She started to turn over, but he stopped her and slid his hand between her legs. She responded to his sign language—fingers pressing against her thighs—and spread them apart. Without saying a word, his finger stroked her bud to life, his strokes slow and easy before easing inside for a more intimate caress. Gliding a finger between the folds of her blossom dripping with dew, brushing her lower-level lips with the lightest touch, squeezing her jewel until it quivered, until she shivered and wondered if one could die from wanting. Amazed at the intensity of the yearning when the last horizontal refreshment was only hours ago.

After she heard the telltale sound of foil tearing, Ike aimed his missile with the precision of a sharpshooter and leisurely sank into her heat. He sighed contentedly and for a few seconds lay there unmoving and took in the moment, keenly aware of all the sensations. His dick pulsed inside her, like a ravenous snake ready to plunder a deep cache for prey. For a minute (or was it an hour?) he thrust and pumped and licked and caressed until Quinn's soft cooing signaled her oncoming release. She was guided to a kneeling position. The snake morphed into a lusty jackhammer, rapid strokes until the heat of their combustion caused a carnal eruption. She whimpered. He hissed. A satiated silence filled the room until they'd both caught their breath.

Ike gently kissed her temple, stroked her hair and said, "Good morning."

Quinn flopped on her back and stretched her hands toward the ceiling. "It's a very good morning! Your dick is so yummy!"

"Quinn…"

"I want to get woken up like that every single day!" She nestled into him, reached for his flaccid member and began bouncing it in her hand.

"What in the world?" Ike grabbed her wrist, sitting up as he moved it.

"What? I'm just playing with it."

"It's not a toy."

"No, it's a machine!"

She looked at him, eyes shining, and started to laugh. He stared back with a scowl. "Come on, Ike. Lighten up!" She reached again for his penis. He blocked her hand. "Let me play with it!"

"Stop!"

"I want it!" She sat up, her breasts bobbing invitingly as she bounced on the bed. "You're acting angry, but I know you want to laugh. You want to. Right?"

She stood and started dancing in the middle of the bed. Stark naked, doing the running man. Ike finally lost control.

"You're insane!"

"You make me crazy." She joined him, sitting with their backs against a beautifully crafted silk-covered headboard. "Do I scare you? Are you starting to wonder what you've gotten into? For the record, you've definitely gotten into something. I can't know there's a dick like that around and not come on the hunt."

"I don't like to hear talk like that."

"Why? That's what it is."

"It's a penis."

"That word sounds yuckier, if you ask me. Okay, I'm sorry. I won't say it anymore. The next time I run into a man named Dick, I'll call him Penis and tell him I had to, because I'm a lady, I am!"

Slipping into an English accent as she ended the sentence cracked them both up.

"Girl, being around you twenty-four-seven would make me crazy!"

"Crazy in love."

"No, crazy in an institution."

"From what I see, you need a little craziness in your life."

The comment genuinely surprised him. "How do you figure?"

"How do I not? A masquerade ball, and your sense of adventure is a black suit and sunglasses. Ooh, daring!"

"Says the woman who walked in naked save a couple of leaves."

"I gave off the appearance of being naked but was covered in what you tore off last night."

"If one looked close enough, they could see your bare ass."

"No, that was later, when I got here and took off my leaves."

"We're opposites in every way."

"That might be a good thing."

Ike slipped an arm around her. "I've never met anyone like you."

"Friends tell me that I'm one of a kind."

"Speaking of friends, tell me about Adam."

"Huh? Oh, you mean Trent. What do you want to know?"

"How'd you meet him?"

"We were both in Switzerland. His cousin and I were in the same school. We both grew up in San Francisco, and with that in common, became good friends. He came to visit. We started talking—he's from the bay, too—and before I knew it we were best friends."

"A friend, not an ex-boyfriend?"

"Ooh, asking those kinds of questions. I think somebody's catching feelings, making sure nobody's dipping in the cookie jar."

Ike remained silent, waited for an answer.

"Trent and I never had sex. We fooled around a little, but that was years ago, when I was still in high school and a virgin. He's bi, and for the last few years has been playing on the other team. So you can stop whatever imaginations are spinning in your head."

"Have you ever had a serious relationship, besides the failed engagement?"

Quinn brought her chin to her knees. It took a while to answer. "I've had relationships where I've really loved the person, but I finally realized that I've never been in love. Does that make sense?"

"I understand completely."

"I'm beginning to understand why. To do so one has to be totally vulnerable. It's hard for me to trust, to open up. I'm afraid of being betrayed, lied to, hurt."

"What happened to make you that way? Judging from your reaction before, it had to be something traumatic."

"My reaction when?"

"When I asked about your mother."

"Oh, that."

"I can't help but be curious. It's my nature, and helps me know more about you. You've met almost everyone in my family. You've even met London! I just want to know who you are."

"Okay."

She said that and nothing more. The room became quiet, lasting so long that Ike wondered if she hadn't fallen asleep.

"I was born on the East Coast, an only child. We lived in a DC suburb."

"Which one?"

"Rockville. Typical middle-class family, I guess. There was an older woman who lived near us, Miss Ruthanne. She'd babysit when Mom had a meeting or event."

"Did your mom work?"

"She was a consultant of some kind, involved in political circles. Always very busy, always on. In every memory I have of her she's very well put together.

"Two weeks before my twelfth birthday, she went to a function in DC. Miss Ruthanne came over. We ate dinner, watched TV. Dad was out of town. The phone rang. Miss Ruthanne answered. I remember her becoming very upset. She must have told me about the accident, but I pretty much shut down after that. Caught bits and pieces. It was winter. Icy roads. Five-car pileup. Two people died.

"My dad shut down, too. He and I are a lot alike in that way. Shortly after everything was over, he took me to my grandmother's house. I didn't see him for three months."

"Was that here? In Paradise Cove?"

Quinn nodded. "She was amazing, my grandmother. Still is. I became very withdrawn, didn't talk much. She enrolled me in ballet classes and arranged music lessons. Violin," she quickly added. "Because you're curious like that."

Ike smiled, reached for her hand and held it.

"Just as the fog of grief was beginning to lift the slightest bit, Dad came back. Announced that San Francisco was our new home, and two days later we were headed to the airport."

"That had to be hard for you. Leaving Mrs. Newman."

"I was sad to leave, but happier that I was with my dad, who by now was more himself. San Francisco was new and fun, like an adventure. I loved our house and my room, which was huge and painted pink and purple with a bay window. Dad hired a nanny with a background in child psychology. Her name was Gloria. She was more on the serious side, like Dad, but encouraging and supportive. On top of losing my mom, I was a hormonal preteen. She helped me navigate that. I knew she genuinely cared about me, even loved me."

"Are the two of you still in touch?"

Quinn shook her head sadly. "I should try to find her. She's probably online. Things changed a year later, but for the time she was in my life, it meant a lot."

"What happened to change things?"

"Dad met Viviana, his current wife. We'd been there for a little over a year, and I was doing a lot better. Dad was always busy but he made time for me, riding bikes, sports, the movies now and then. And we'd eat out. On one particular Sunday, he said we were going out to eat and to get dressed up. That was a little different. It was usually a casual thing. But I was excited. I thought we were doing something special or he had a surprise. I didn't know. But I was game.

"We arrived at the restaurant and were seated. That's when he informed me that someone was going to join us. A little while later this woman approaches our table—beautiful, elegant. I disliked her immediately. The feeling was mutual. She said the right things, smiled the right way, but I could feel that it wasn't genuine. She wanted my father.

He was a package deal. So I was tolerated. Six months later, the wedding of the decade took place at Bentley Reserve. You're probably familiar with it?"

"Very much so. One of the financial district's oldest and most prominent landmarks."

"By the time they returned from an extended honeymoon, Dad was wrapped around her finger. He went back to work, she became the woman of the house and everything changed."

"How?"

"Replacing Gloria with someone I believe served as her watchdog. For me that was yet another loss. The household became formal and highbrow. I rebelled, which is probably exactly what she wanted. Because a year later, I was in Switzerland and she had my dad the way she'd always wanted him, all to herself."

"How is the relationship now between you and your dad?"

"Strained. Distant. Not much communication between us in the past five or so years."

"Quinn! He's your father. How can that happen?"

"Like I said, we're a lot alike. Grandmother says that's why the stalemate has gone on so long. She's right. At times I was horrible and put Dad through a lot. But I love him. And I want him in my life. So I'm going to reach out."

"Good for you." He raised her hand to his lips and kissed it. "I'm really glad to hear you say that."

Quinn faced Ike more fully, her gaze filled with admiration…even awe. "You want to know something? Your family is part of the reason. Seeing how all of you interact when together. Working together, the love that's so obvious. And the respect. I've never experienced that, and I must admit… I'm a little jealous."

"Don't be jealous. There's enough love to go around."

He pulled her close and let his lips give her an idea of how much. She melted into his embrace, but just as his hands began to roam she sat back, moved to widen the distance between them.

"Sweetheart, what is it?"

"Ike…there's something I need to tell you, and you're not going to like it."

Chapter 21

Quinn wanted to tell him and get it over with. But when he heard the topic was business, he insisted on going downstairs for something to eat. "Never discuss money when your stomach's empty," he joked. But she saw concern in his eyes.

They showered together, then went to the kitchen. Ike wore a pair of loose workout pants, the band settling around his hips. Clearly in his domain, he methodically assembled items for an omelet and began preparations.

Quinn had on one of Ike's sleeveless T-shirts. On her, it looked like a dress. She poured juice into two glasses, retrieved plates and silverware, then settled at island. For ten excruciating minutes, she engaged in small talk while Ike cooked. When silent, she mentally weighed the options of how best to break this news. Finally, with a fluffy vegetable omelet before her and twice the amount on Ike's plate, he said, "Okay, talk."

"How thoroughly did your company vet Global 100?"

Ike's reaction showed the question caught him off guard. *As completely as we do all companies with which we do business.* They'd checked multiple references, financial statements, extensive background checks and a few other measures. As investors who stood to gain a considerable profit but would have no ownership in the building, the most important information Global 100 was regarding their financials and the ability to successfully assist in funding this deal. And everything checked out. "Why? Is what you're wanting to share about our partner?"

"Yes."

Ike paused, looking slightly amused as he drank orange juice. "And you believe it's information I'll find upsetting?"

"Yes, Ike. For several reasons, this news is not good."

Her serious countenance sobered Ike's mood. He rested his fork on the plate and gave Quinn his undivided attention. "I'm listening."

"This information isn't public knowledge. It isn't something that would be discovered through a vetting process. But it comes from a very reliable source, a person who ended his relationship with the company when he learned how their wealth is obtained. Behind the scenes, far enough to be invisible, are deposed military leaders, corrupt politicians, including heads of state, and dictatorial bullies who use their countries' riches as their own for financial gain. All while citizens starve, infrastructures crumble…and people die!" Repeating what Trent had told her fueled Quinn's ire. Though the circumstances were different, she knew how it felt to be treated unjustly.

"They've hired what my friend called suits. Men to run the business and make the deals, who present the right corporate image. But behind that facade is a group of narcissists fueled by greed. This person cut ties with Global 100 because, in his words, 'their money dripped blood.'"

Quinn sat back, drained by the gravity of what she'd shared and wary of Ike's reaction. For a whole minute, at least, there was none. He studied her, then looked away, his expression unreadable. This was the Ike with whom she was more familiar—deliberate, judicious, controlled. Her nerves grew raw. She was anxious, desperate to know what was on his mind. Was he in shock at hearing this news for the very first time, his mind grappling with the enormity of its implications? Had she relayed information Ike and his family already knew? Suddenly, a thought occurred to her—if the Drakes were in bed with this international band of creeps, she'd just spilled secrets no one should know but the company COO. One partnered with el creepos in a one-hundred-million-dollar deal. While sitting in his kitchen, alone save for him and a block of knives displayed on the counter.

Every crime show she'd ever watched flashed into her mind. What had seemed like the only solution half an hour ago now felt like a very bad idea.

Ike stretched his arms upward before clasping them behind his head. The sudden movement made Quinn flinch. Ike didn't notice, his mind obviously preoccupied.

"Wow," he finally uttered. "Just when I thought you couldn't possibly shock me any more than you have already, I get proved wrong completely. It's clear from your passion that you believe what this friend told you."

"Like I said, the source is very credible."

"Who is it?" Quinn didn't respond. "Confidentiality aside, of course. Assuming it was a discussion about Ten Drake Plaza that precipitated this conversation, my being informed is appropriate."

What if revealing Trent's identity, or that of his father, put them in danger? What if one of the gangsters got wind that she knew and came to PC? She could get kidnapped! Quinn's imagination spiraled out of control. Maggie had warned her that watching the Investigation Discovery channel wasn't good for her health.

"Are you all right?"

"Yes. I need to ask a question, and I hope you answer truthfully."

"I will."

"Did you know any of what I just shared? About who is funding Global and benefiting the most from their profits?"

Ike began to frown. The longer he pondered her question, the more it deepened.

"Of course not. How could you even think that question, let alone ask it?"

"I'd never want to believe anything like that, but I had

to ask. Dangerous people and billions of dollars can be a very dangerous mix."

"True, but I would have hoped the time you've spent with my family would make such a question moot."

"I'm sorry. And I'm probably overthinking and overreacting, but I'm protecting people I love." She paused a few seconds and then said, "It's my best friend, Trent."

"You discussed Drake company business with him?"

"Not intentionally. Before Trent arrived in Paradise Cove, we hadn't seen each other for months. Hadn't talked much. We were both so excited, ready to catch up on each other's lives. He shared what was happening in his world. I told him mine. How the accident resulted in me working with you and reviewing a report, and how good it felt to actually use some of what I learned in school. And somewhere in the middle of all of that their name was mentioned."

"What kind of business deal was it?"

"Deal?"

"Yes. What were Trent's business dealings with Global?"

"It wasn't Trent who dealt with them. It was his father."

"His father is in real estate?"

"No. His father is Phillip Corrigan, the former president of Compliance National, the financial district branch."

Thirty minutes later, Quinn was on her way home via town car. Ike was in his home office, searching the internet and poring over files. He found nothing that came close to substantiating any of what Quinn claimed. But what she'd said could not be dismissed. Quinn's passion lent credibility. The Corrigan name further legitimized it.

Ike checked his watch, then reached for the phone. It was early afternoon. No doubt the Drakes' Sunday brunch was in full effect. This information was too volatile to share by phone. He quickly placed his tablet and a few pertinent documents in his briefcase. After a quick look around, he snatched his car keys from the hook and was out the door.

His home was less than five minutes away from where his parents resided. He reached the cul-de-sac quickly but just before turning into it made an abrupt change in plans. This volatile information would no doubt elicit a variety of actions and likely bring on a debate in how to proceed. The closing on Ten Drake Plaza was days away. There was no time to lose. Ike made an executive decision on gut instinct alone. He'd meet with Bernard Lindsay of Global 100 and if necessary, then involve the team. No need to get everyone stirred up over what may be a wild goose chase. Once through the gates and out of the community, Ike engaged his phone. The first call went to voice mail. He left a message and tapped another name.

"Mr. Drake. What can I do for you?"

"Hello, Stan. I hate to bother you on a Sunday, but something's come up, rather important. I need to make a quick trip to San Francisco."

"Sure thing, Mr. Drake. How soon would you like to travel?"

"As soon as you can get the plane ready. I'm headed to the airport now."

When he landed in San Francisco, the whirlwind continued. Ike exited the plane, got into a waiting limo and pulled out his phone. It rang in his hand.

"Mr. Lindsay, how are you?"

"Life is good, Drake. What about yourself?"

"Doing fine. No complaints."

"That's good to hear, especially considering the tone of your message. It sounded urgent."

"Probably sounded a little more serious than it actually is, but I happen to be here in the bay and wanted to meet with you briefly, if possible. I know it's Sunday, but it is a matter I'd like to clear up."

"Can you give me an idea of what this is about?"

"I'd prefer to speak privately. It's probably nothing. But since I'm here..."

"Of course. Where are you?"

"Not too far from Pier 39."

"I'm about twenty minutes from that area. There's a little-known spot just below where the tourists gather, a small platform that juts out over the water. It'll give us privacy. I'll text the directions."

"See you then, man."

Ike reached the area Bernard had suggested, quiet and secluded, as he'd described. It was cold, in the forties, the sun bright. Even so, Ike perspired. He removed his suit coat, closed his eyes and breathed in the ocean's salty mist. The air was clean and crisp. His nerves settled down. From this calm place, away from Quinn's passion, the story sounded impossible, almost ludicrous. Yet he'd jumped on a plane, pulled two men from their families and stood waiting to question a fifty-million-dollar partner about invisible ties to corruption and greed. By the time Bernard arrived fifteen minutes later, Ike wished he hadn't made the trip.

Bernard Lindsay was all smiles as he sauntered toward Ike—trench coat blowing in the wind, a black fedora tipped to a jaunty angle, wing-tipped shoes shined spotless. The picture of financial success.

"Mr. Drake," Bernard boomed with hand outstretched.

"Mr. Lindsay. Thank you so much for agreeing to meet on such a short notice."

"No problem at all, Ike. The closing's coming up. This thing's about to get real. It's understandable that last-minute questions might arise." He motioned toward a wrought-iron bench. "Let's sit down and discuss what's on your mind."

They strolled casually, even as Ike struggled for a way to handle this situation without coming off as a total idiot.

"Ah, man." Bernard sighed as he sat, and ran a hand over his face. "I've got to stop burning the candle at both ends. The body doesn't bounce back at forty-five the way it did at twenty-five."

"I won't know about that for another ten years."

"That's right. Forgot you're a youngster."

"I'm not going to hold you up, Bernard. In fact, the more I've thought about it—" he chuckled and shook his head "—we probably could have spoken by phone and saved you the trip. I guess the pressure of everything coming together has me paranoid."

"I'm here now, brother. So bring it on."

Ike looked out at the water as he spoke, embarrassed to face this respected businessman with speculation. "I can't believe I'm even repeating this. Recently, I received information that, if true, would have serious repercussions. That's if it were true. According to this source, Global has international partners not disclosed in official company documents, unscrupulous men with dirty money who are the actual funders behind the billion-dollar asset sheet. Highly improbable, I know, but—" Ike laughed again, more gregariously this time, to emphasize his personal disbelief of the tale.

He sat back, expecting to see Bernard's signature smile and endure a ribbing. There was no smile. Bernard Lindsay was all business.

"The problem, Mr. Drake, is that confidential information appears to have been discussed."

"Not at all. Circles are small. People talk. One needn't know of a partnership to share what they've heard. I found it intriguing but unlikely, as I stated. I can't see you or the other partners being puppets for an illegal operation funded by criminals."

"You are correct. I am neither a puppet, nor a criminal and I resent the merest implication of such."

"I have not called you either," Ike replied, intrigued by Bernard's reaction. "Nor have I given undo credence to what I heard. But surely you can understand my need to mention it, at the very least, and eliminate the slightest of chances that it's true."

"It's not true."

Ike nodded slowly, eyeing Bernard as he did so and

checking his gut. The relief he thought would come from the answer he'd hoped for did not happen.

"I am relieved to hear that," he said. "I've always believed you to be a stand up man, Bernard. Your answer is no surprise."

Bernard stood. "I apologize for having to cut this meeting short. But if there is nothing else to discuss, I need to get back to an engagement."

"Certainly." Ike stood as well, his hand extended. Bernard accepted the handshake but did not meet Ike's eye. Ike's gut rumbled.

"If I could get you to do one more thing for me, this matter will be totally put to bed. I need a statement on company letterhead, attesting to what you just confirmed, that there are no other partners or financial contributors—silent, invisible or otherwise—that have not been documented and that if audited, all monies could be accounted for from the sources listed in that documentation."

Bernard's eyes narrowed. "Interesting request from one who considers me a standup guy."

"A matter of documentation is all."

"Who've you been talking to?"

"Obviously someone who didn't have their facts straight. If that letter can be notarized and couriered to my office tomorrow, I'll consider this matter closed."

"Global 100 has provided all required documentation for this transaction. This matter is closed now."

"Why such resistance to a simple request?"

"He who has the money, calls the shots." He turned and left without another word.

Ike watched Bernard's retreat with an uneasy feeling, followed by a thought that chilled him to the bone.

What if all he'd heard was true?

He left the pier and headed straight for the airport. On the way, he called his dad.

"Hello, son. Your mother talked you up. Wondering what kept you away from brunch."

"Wondering *who*," Jennifer corrected from the background.

"I was handling some business, Dad. In fact, I'm in San Francisco now, on my way back to PC."

"San Francisco? What's going on?"

"That's what we need to figure out. I'm calling an emergency family meeting, Dad, ninety minutes from now."

Chapter 22

Ike arrived at his parents' home just a couple minutes past the time he'd set for the meeting. He was pleased to see all of the siblings currently in Paradise Cove represented by the cars in the drive. As daunting as the meeting before him was, he looked forward to being surrounded by family. No matter what else happened, he could count on his clan for moral support. The meeting with Bernard Lindsay had left him feeling no love at all.

He bopped up the steps and entered the house. It was quiet. Deathly so. For the second time today, the hairs on his neck stood at attention. The family knew nothing of what he was about to share. What could possibly have happened in the past ninety minutes that made this usually warm, vibrant house feel like a morgue?

The low rumble of his father's voice traveled down the hall as Ike neared the great room. Two steps in, and he was stopped in his tracks. The tableau was of the Drake family, but the mood was all wrong. His mother, always the first to greet him with a smile and a kiss, sat with her head slightly bowed. Jokester Terrell stood near the window, failing to deliver the quip Ike expected about working overtime. Warren and Niko sat on the couch. His father in an armchair. Except for the actions of two people, Ike would have sworn he'd turned invisible, unable to be detected as he walked into the room. Warren looked up. Their eyes met briefly before he looked away. And his father fixed him with a look that Ike had no time to interpret. He didn't have to.

"Ike Jr.," his father intoned as he stood. "What in the hell have you done?"

The anger in Ike Sr.'s voice took him aback. But only for a second. "That's what I'm here to explain."

"That won't be necessary," Warren offered.

Terrell finally looked at him and sneered. "You've said enough."

Back roared confusion, along with mounting fear. "I called this meeting for a very legitimate reason, but it is clear that between then and my arrival, something else has taken place. What is it?"

"Global 100 has pulled their financing," Terrell answered. "The deal is off the table."

The news hit Ike like an actual blow. He ambled over to a nearby loveseat and plopped down.

Terrell walked past, sneer still in place. "Thought that might get your attention."

Niko walked over and sat next to Ike. "Everyone is in shock, bro, unable to believe what just happened. Having no idea what happened, really. I know how you operate. You're not the kind of person to go off half-cocked or to act with misinformation. I'm sure there is a compelling explanation for what took place between you and Bernard."

Terrell snorted. "Whatever it was sank a deal in five minutes that took five years to build."

So that was it. Bernard had dropped the bomb Ike had planned to deliver. It must have exploded minutes before he arrived. He'd walked in and caught shrapnel, and it was still falling. That the deal was over was something Ike couldn't yet contemplate. The whole situation was a minefield. He took a breath instead of a step, and hoped not to blow up.

"I'm not sure what spin Bernard put on my visit, but this is what actually happened. Earlier, I received extremely unsettling news concerning Global 100, news that came from a reliable source who'd done business with them in the past before learning what was shared with me and cutting all ties."

"From whom?" Ike Sr. demanded.

"Quinn relayed the information, but it came from Phillip Corrigan."

"Quinn?" Terrell asked incredulously.

"Did you speak directly to Phillip?" Ike, Sr. strode toward Ike.

"No, but—"

"And yet you took it upon yourself, without a word to the other company execs, to fly to San Francisco and deliver malicious and unfounded accusations to his face."

"That's not what happened."

"That's how he interpreted whatever took place. You weren't the only one calling a meeting. While you were in the air, he obviously called one, too. They broke contract on the clause concerning confidentiality, because even though anonymously you mentioned a source not connected with this transaction, it's over. Done. Just like that."

Ike eased back against the couch. His mind whirled. Bernard's actions didn't make sense, and he said as much.

"No, brother. What you did doesn't make sense, s-e-n-s-e," Terrell quipped, spelling it out so there'd be no mistaking what he said. "But because of it, every c-e-n-t of their investment is gone."

"I know it's hard to do, but I'm asking all of you to hear me out, then decide for yourselves which reaction was reasonable—Bernard Lindsay's or mine."

An hour later, Ike was in his office at Drake Realty, scrolling his address book for contacts who might have done business with Global 100. At Jennifer's insistence, his dad and brothers had listened to the report he'd been given. They'd agreed the accusations were horrendous but also felt that for the most part they were too outrageous to be true. Terrell was the angriest. He believed the whole story was hogwash and conveyed his disappointment at Ike's lack of restraint. Warren's beef, and that of his father, was that he'd gone against company policy and acted alone. Every major move, and most minor ones, were discussed by all execs. Niko didn't reject the possibility outright, believing few politicians could be trusted. Even though he was one. The only real encouragement came from his mother.

"Quinn's a bright girl," she'd offered as she walked him to the door. "She wouldn't share something so significant without good reason. Ask for her assistance. If you believe what she told you, keep searching to prove the truth and don't give up."

On the way to the office, he'd followed his mother's advice and left a message on Quinn's voice mail when she didn't answer. Jennifer was right. Quinn's help could be crucial. If given the chance to meet with Phillip Corrigan, Ike could confirm the story and feel he'd done the right thing. Or find no truth to what she'd said and never forgive himself.

When the face of Ike's phone lit up with her calling, he answered before it had a chance to ring.

"Ike! Your message sounded serious. What's going on?"

"A hailstorm of problems. I'm at the office. Can you come over? It's important."

"Sure. I'm on my way."

Ike didn't know why the thought of Quinn coming over made him feel so much better. She was partly why he was in this predicament. But it did.

When she texted her arrival, Ike moved quickly to let her in. Barely through the door, he pulled her into his arms, soaked up the comfort found in her embrace. Crazy—he couldn't explain it, but being in her arms felt like home.

"I've been worried since this morning and what I shared. Then I called you and when I didn't get an answer, became more concerned. What's the matter?"

"You called me?"

"Yes, around eleven or twelve, I guess."

"I was on a flight but that shouldn't have mattered."

"You flew somewhere and are back already? Where'd you go?"

"Come into my office. I'll tell you all about it."

He did, ending with the grand flourish of the fallen deal. "The family is ready to disown me. But there's something to what you told me. I feel it in my gut."

"How can I help?"

Ike looked up from his phone, the warmth in his eyes enough to boil water. "I'm glad you asked. I need to meet with Phillip Corrigan. Get the information firsthand, the proof of what is happening and why doing business with that group is not an option."

"I can try, but I don't know if it's possible."

"Why not? You told me Trent is your best friend."

"Trent told me his dad became extremely unnerved during the time he dealt with Global 100. He didn't share the specifics, might not even know them. But I guess there were some pretty serious threats, and strong encouragement not to talk about what he suspected or had uncovered. Trent believes it's part of the reason his parents now spend most of their time in Idaho, in a beautiful but rather remote location. But I will try, and share whatever is uncovered when I come in tomorrow."

"Your four-week stint is over."

"Yes, but Lydia asked for a couple more days, just to tie things up."

"Your coming in is not a good idea, sweetheart. Nothing personal, but you're not my family's favorite person right now. Let me take the heat while you work on getting to Corrigan. Do that, and I'll take back everything I said after you wrecked my Ferrari."

Chapter 23

Later that evening, after another quick tryst with Ike, Quinn returned home and called Trent, who'd returned to Paris. She shared scant details on what happened and relayed Ike's request.

"I don't know, Q-Tip. I told you how weird Dad is about that whole thing. Just knowing I shared it with you would probably freak him out."

"I told Ike it might not be easy. But I feel partly responsible for what happened. I share a story and a building falls down. Like I'm walking around with cloud calamity over my head. If I could somehow help to salvage the deal…"

"Hey."

"What?"

"Now, that may be a way to get to my dad."

"How?"

"Cut him in on the deal."

"Seriously? You think he'd be an investor?"

"I don't know, but that's a safer conversation than the one you proposed. And then perhaps segue into Global talk from there. But I think he'd be open to a discussion with you, Quinn, instead of a company executive. You're like his other kid. He'd feel comfortable and be more likely to open up with you."

"Are your parents in San Francisco or Idaho?"

"San Francisco, I think. But I'm not sure. I'll give you Dad's cell number and you can take it from there."

"If I can make something happen, this would be huge! Thank you, Trench Coat. I love you, bestie."

"You're welcome, Q-Tip. I love you, too."

Quinn wasted no time. She ended the call and without time to think about it, dialed a San Francisco number. She gripped the phone, awaiting an answer. He picked up.

"Hi, Dad."

"Quinn?"

"Yes. I guess it's no surprise you don't recognize my voice. It's been a while."

"Of course I recognize you, honey. I'm surprised, that's all. But pleasantly so. How are you, Quinn?"

"I'm good, for the most part."

"What's going on with those parts that aren't so good?"

"Just personal stuff—more life classes."

"Those are some of the toughest, but often some of the best. How's Mom?"

"She's good. The doctor changed her medication and the arthritis is better. I think it's time to talk about some live-in assistance for her."

"Are you planning to move?"

"Not right this moment, but at some point."

"I guess that town's too small for you."

"It's all right. I even had the opportunity to put my Ivy League education to use."

"Really? How so?"

Quinn shared the experience of working at Drake Realty Plus. "That's actually what has indirectly led to this call. I'm planning a trip to San Francisco and wanted to see you."

"Absolutely! I've missed you, honey."

"I know. Me, too. I finally started opening up about… everything. I really want to talk with you about it."

"Text me the details of your visit and we'll make plans from there."

"Okay."

"I love you, Kristin Quinn."

"I love you, Dad."

On a roll, she called Phillip Corrigan and made plans to see him, too.

Her flight landed the next day at noon. With only a carry-on, she was quickly out of the airport and on her way to the Corrigans' home in Pacific Heights.

She arrived and with Phillip's boisterous greeting was transported back to the age of sixteen and their first meeting in Switzerland. His constant teasing made her blush. Not much had changed.

"There she is! Honey! Sound the bugles. Queen Quinn has arrived!"

"Hello, Mr. Corrigan." She fell into his outstretched arms for his famous bear hug. He was a big man, around six-three, with a growing paunch and more gray than she remembered, but otherwise still the same man.

"Let me look at you. My goodness, how long has it been?"

"Five years, at least?"

"That long? Come on in. The wife's around here somewhere, probably getting the cook to whip up something decadent that none of us need. Sit down. Take a load off."

Instead Quinn was drawn to the large picture window. "What an incredible view! You can see forever. The bridge, downtown—this is stunning. The entire home, in fact."

"Yeah, my bank account said the same thing."

"Now, Phillip, let's not ruin a girl's fantasy with the details. Hello, dear."

"Hi, Mrs. Corrigan." They hugged.

"It's so good to see you. I have a Swiss treat being prepared, just in case you want to nibble."

They settled into the beautifully appointed living room.

"So tell us, Quinn. What's going on in your life?"

For the next two hours, Quinn caught them up-to-date. She left without discussing Global 100 but had piqued Mr. Corrigan's curiosity about Ten Drake Plaza. The thought of helping the Drakes secure financing was exciting. But she'd learned her lesson and would share this development with no one until Mr. Corrigan was fully on board and ready to meet with Ike.

Quinn gazed at the passing scenery on the way to her father's town house in the tony area of Presidio Heights. Purchased after downsizing two years ago, it would be her first time to his and Viviana's new home. The thought of Viviana led to unpleasant memories, and to Quinn wondering how life would be if her mother was alive. She vanquished the thought before it could form fully. The visit would already be hard enough.

They reached the Taylor residence. Quinn paid the car service and walked with the driver to the front door, where he deposited the carry-on he'd insisted on handling, made a last flirty comment and left. Quinn took a breath and rang the bell. She was expecting her father, but instead Viviana opened the door.

"Hello, Quinn. Come right in out of the cold."

"Hello." Quinn reached for the luggage handle and rolled it inside.

"Just leave it there, dear. The staff will deliver it to your room. You can leave your coat as well. Remove your shoes and choose a pair of booties from the chest."

Quinn did as instructed. "Is Dad here?"

"Not at the moment. He was called away unexpectedly but wanted me to assure you that he'll be back soon. In fact, we have dinner reservations for six thirty. In the meantime, we can get you settled, prepare a snack if you're hungry, or perhaps you'd like to take a nap—whatever you need."

"Thanks."

"Let's adjourn to the informal living room, shall we? I was just having a cup of tea. May I have one brought to you?"

"That's okay. I can go to the guest room and get settled in."

"Actually, Quinn, I'd very much like to speak with you, if I may. It needn't be long. Just five or ten minutes, maybe?"

"Okay."

"Are you sure I can't talk you into joining me for tea? I first received it as a gift, and after finishing the box began ordering it on my own. It is the most divine blend of citrus and spices. I've become quite addicted."

Even her laughter was cultured. Not even a laugh. A titter. Soft and melodic, perfectly pitched, delivered through unmoving lips. Quinn would have much rather retreated to the guest room and social media, but it was obvious Viviana was trying. So she'd try, too.

"Sure. I'll join you."

"Perfect." While Viviana spoke to the maid, Quinn sat in one of two empire chairs. After rattling off a list of instructions, she sat in the other one and offered what Quinn felt was a sincere smile.

"So...how was your flight?"

"Uneventful." True answer, but Quinn knew it was not a proper one. If her social graces instructor back in Switzerland could hear her, she would be very disappointed. "That was a good thing," she continued after clearing her throat, "because there is a cold front sweeping across Denver that has caused cancellations."

"Isn't this unseasonably cold weather dreadful? I'm a San Franciscan born and bred, but I've never gotten used to the cold. This year, spending the holidays in Marmorata. I simply can't wait. We've only planned a month's stay, and your father has obligations toward the end of January, but I just may have to extend my visit until spring."

Viviana tittered. Quinn returned a small smile. It was the best she do. Neither Viviana nor her father had an obligation to invite her along. They were married, she was grown and they all had their own lives. She probably would have declined, but having the invitation extended would have been nice.

The maid brought in a tray of tea and finger sandwiches. A few silent minutes were spent flavoring their teas. Viviana took a sip and gently set down her cup.

"Quinn, I know our relationship has not been ideal."

Not ideal? It's been nonexistent.

"I bear some of the blame for that. Never having had children or spent much time around them, I didn't consider your feelings the way that I should have. I'm ashamed to say that to even look at the situation from your point of view never crossed my mind. I'd survived a horrendous marriage and a divorce worse than that. Meeting Glen was like seeing sunshine after an Alaskan winter, with no light at all, and I was like a flower that had survived a drought. He was—and still is, quite frankly—the center of my universe. Unlike any man I've ever met before. Back then, during our courtship and right after we married, I wanted him to be as consumed with me as I was with him. I wanted all of his attention and I made selfish choices that were to your detriment."

"No, you made selfish demands. My father made the choice to give in to them."

"In his defense, I can be quite persuasive—some would use less flattering terms—when I want to get my way. He wanted you here, Quinn, in San Francisco. I wore him down, and when you understandably began acting out, I offered the perfect solution. One where I'd have Glen's total focus."

"You're why I was sent to school in Switzerland?"

Viviana nodded slowly. "I have friends who'd sent their children there and spoke of it highly. It's a great school in a beautiful setting. But it wasn't life with your parent, your father. I want to apologize, Quinn. I'm so sorry for coming between you and Glen, and for contributing to the breakdown in your relationship. I won't ask now, but I hope that someday you'll be able to forgive me, and that if we can't be friends, that we can at least be friendly."

"Thank you, Viviana. It doesn't change what happened, but your apology means a lot."

Glen came home two hours later, surprised to see Quinn and Viviana laughing and talking together as they sipped glasses of wine.

"Hold it. No, stay right there," he told them, reaching into his briefcase to pull out his cell phone. "I want to capture this happy moment between the two women I love most in the world." He aimed his smartphone and quickly took at least a dozen shots. "All right, ladies, give me a moment to freshen up and we'll head to dinner."

"Actually, dear, something's come up and I won't be able to join you."

"What is it?" Glen asked, concerned.

"Nothing to worry about, Glen. You two go on and enjoy each other. It's been a while since that's happened. I'm sure there's a great deal to share."

Viviana gave Glen a hug and kiss, then turned and hugged Quinn, a rarity. With a quick wink, she left the room.

Quinn realized what she'd done and was grateful.

"Well, honey. It's just the two of us. Shall we?"

Quinn threaded her arm through her father's and, for the first time since she was twelve years old, felt like daddy's little girl.

The restaurant was less than five miles away from Judge Taylor's impressive zip code, straight down California Street. Traffic could be brutal on this popular road, but not tonight. They arrived at the restaurant ten minutes later and were seated right away. During the ride and for the first few minutes after sitting down, conversation was minimal. But the silence didn't feel awkward. For both father and daughter, after so many years away of strained interactions, just sitting and basking in their mutual love felt better than any words could convey.

Quinn studied Pabu's diverse menu of tasty-sounding items. It was her first time at the restaurant, but its stellar food and drink list was not a surprise. Her father had always enjoyed the finer things of life and had passed this taste down to his daughter. As her mouth watered, Quinn realized why every item described sounded amazing. Besides the cheese fondue the Corrigans' chef had prepared as an homage to Switzerland, and a few treats she'd enjoyed during Viviana's afternoon tea, Quinn hadn't eaten a thing. Tonight she would enjoy the company and the food.

"Dad, how—" What Quinn saw when she looked up stopped her speech. Were those tears? She'd never seen her dad cry in her entire life. Not even at her mom's funeral. "What's wrong, Dad?"

Glen smiled and allowed the tear that quivered at the side of his eye to run down his cheek. "Nothing's wrong, baby. Your father's just happy, that's all. Tonight, everything feels right."

"Oh, Dad!" Quinn left her seat to come around and hug her father. She wrapped her arms around his shoulders and laid her cheek on his head. His shoulders shook beneath her embrace as the dam holding back decades of tears crumbled and he allowed the tears to flow. Quinn felt her own eyes begin to water and ended the embrace. She returned to her seat, reached for linen napkin and dabbed the corners of her eyes. "I've never seen you cry," she admitted to her father.

"It doesn't happen often." With his emotions in control once again, Glen pulled a handkerchief from an inside suit pocket and wiped his face. "I can't even remember the last time. Watching you just now took me back ten, fifteen years, to the times I saw your mother looking that exact same way."

"I always thought I looked more like you."

"You definitely have the more prominent Taylor features. Your body type, nose, eyes. But I see a lot of Brenda in you, too, especially your mannerisms—even some of your personality is like hers. In hindsight, I think that's why I left you with Mom after she died. You were such a reminder of all I'd lost."

"I missed you so much then, Dad. I needed you. I was hurting, too!"

"I know, baby. That's why I've apologized and reached out to you so many times. But being like your father, you didn't want to deal with it, either, didn't want to revisit the past. So I finally left you alone to sort it out in your own way. But I always hoped for this moment, when we could find our way back to how it used to be."

"Viviana apologized today." Judge Taylor nodded. "That meant a lot."

"I can't tell you what it did for me to see the two of you together and actually getting along."

"I was pretty shocked."

Glen's deep laughter bubbled up from his chest. He waved away the waiter as he sat back to hear his daughter out.

"She took you away from me. That's how I felt."

"That was my fault. When your mother died, when I lost Brenda, I went numb. Honestly, I didn't know how to live without her. We'd begun dating in our teens. It was like she was always in my life. We had so many plans, big ones, and spent so much time working to make them come true—and looking back, not as much time together. Just enjoying each other, being a family.

"I blamed myself for her death. Irrational, but that's what happened. It's why I took it so hard. I went through all of the coulda, shoulda, wouldas, and then I shut down. I was a broken man. That's the other reason why I left you in Paradise Cove. It isn't a way a father wants his daughter to see him.

"When I met Viviana, I was still lost, burying everything beneath a crushing workload. She took the lead in the relationship, and without my even asking or telling her how, put order back into my life. She was my buoy in a sea of nothingness. I clung to her. And lost you in the process."

"I had no idea."

"I know."

"We were both hurting."

"Yes."

Quinn reached across the table. Glen squeezed her hand.

"I love you, Dad. I hope we can do this again, you know, every now and then. Just you and me."

"We can do it whenever you want, baby. I want us to have a lifetime of moments like these."

Chapter 24

Instead of the in-and-out twenty-four-hour trip she'd planned, Quinn stayed at her father's house for three days. It would have been longer, except her grandmother developed a nasty cold and Quinn wanted to be there for her.

There'd been one other rather significant change in plans. Instead of using her return ticket, Quinn drove the roughly 120 miles between San Francisco and Paradise Cove in the surprise gift her father had presented the night before—a fully loaded Corvette Stingray convertible, with a custom pearl-white body and burgundy top. Heads turned as she entered Paradise Cove, her music blasting, her foot on the gas, pushing the boundaries of the posted speed limits. She pulled into Maggie's driveway exhilarated from the drive and, more, from time with her father. The woman who'd left Paradise Cove was not the same woman who returned. Quinn had boarded the plane with a hole in her heart that had now been filled with forgiveness and love.

Along with the carry-on, her sole outbound luggage, Quinn entered her home with three pieces, two filled with new clothes.

"Kristin Quinn!" Maggie was lying on the couch under an afghan but sat up when she heard the door open. "It looks as though you bought out all of San Francisco."

"Not hardly," Quinn replied, sitting in the Queen Anne chair and pulling the luggage closer. "But I did go shopping. With Viviana."

The whoop from Maggie was the reaction she'd expected. "My heavens, child. Was that at gunpoint?"

"Ha! Anyone who knows our history would think that a reasonable response. This visit was different. It was unlike any other time I've spent with her, or with all of us, including Dad."

"When you called to say you'd extended the trip, I knew there was a story behind it."

"I didn't realize how much I missed my father until we were back together. You were right. About everything. Talking about Mom has helped me heal. The exact opposite of what I thought would happen, of what seemed to occur in the past. And about reaching out to Dad. Letting go of past hurts. Practicing forgiveness. The change was amazing and happened so quickly. It's almost as if it began the moment I decided to forgive Dad, even before it actually happened."

Maggie's eyes beamed. "Yes, dear. That's how it works."

Quinn shared the initial conversation she'd had with Viviana, and how she'd acknowledged her errors and apologized.

"I'd never thought about asking for an apology. But it felt good to get one. What totally floored me was when she excused herself from dinner so Dad and I could go alone."

"She did?"

"I couldn't believe it, either. She said something had come up but then winked at me when Dad wasn't looking. So I know she did it for me. I can't believe I'm saying this, Grandmother, but she and Dad have been married ten years. By their fifteenth anniversary, I might even like her."

"Quinn..."

"Just teasing, Grandmother. I don't think we'll ever be best buds. Being cordial and able to share a room without tension is huge enough."

"It's a place to start."

"I also visited the Corrigans, Trent's parents."

"That had to have been nice."

"It was. I hadn't seen them in years."

"Discuss anything interesting?"

"Just caught up on each other's lives," Quinn responded before changing the subject once again.

"In case you were under the misimpression that my shopping was all self-centered—" she pulled out one of the larger boxes "—this is for you."

"Quinn, you're such a sweetheart. You shouldn't have gone to the trouble."

"I absolutely should have, and I loved every minute."

Maggie was thrilled with the dresses, scarves and jewelry Quinn had chosen. "I think these gifts have healing powers. I feel all better."

Quinn felt better, too. But one matter prevented her complete happiness—her part in the failed purchase of Ten Drake Plaza. If that situation could be turned around, and she and Ike could get back the feelings they'd shared the weekend of the masquerade ball, her world would be perfect and all of her dreams would have come true.

Ike resisted the urge to slam down the receiver. He gripped it tightly, let a couple seconds pass and then placed it gently back on the cradle. It was the third time he'd attempted to speak with Bernard. Obviously the businessman had been offended at what Ike's comments implied. But his reaction was over-the-top. Ike wanted to know why.

Pushing back from his desk, he walked over to his door and closed it. He went to the window, a place where some of this best thinking occurred. He watched as PC residents went about their normal lives, unaware and unconcerned that Ike's had been shaken off its foundation. This was unfamiliar territory. It hadn't taken Ike long to realize that it was a position he didn't care for and didn't handle well.

It was a beautiful day, temperatures in the high sixties, not a cloud in the sky. Deciding he'd benefit from a break and fresh air, Ike grabbed his cell phone, forwarded his calls to Lydia and left the building. He crossed the street and headed north, no particular destination in mind. What he'd actually like would be to run away from this nightmare, but that was not an option with the last name Drake. Drakes didn't cower. Drakes didn't run. Drakes met challenges, opponents, life, head-on. It's what had been passed down for at least three generations. If he was blessed to have them, it was a lesson he'd teach his children, as well.

He reached the intersection where the accident with Quinn had occurred, crossed the street and passed the local florist shop. On a whim, he went inside. Bernard wasn't the only person hard to reach. Since leaving with Quinn the night of the ball, Audrey had refused his calls as well and not responded to texts. Maybe a bouquet of flowers delivered to her job would let her know there were no hard feelings. In fact, he felt her actions were justified and what he deserved.

"Good afternoon, sir. May I help you?"

"Yes. I'm looking for a beautiful bouquet of flowers."

"You've come to the right place. What's the occasion? Birthday? Anniversary?"

"No special occasion, actually. These are for a good friend who can use some cheering up."

"That's very thoughtful of you. Does he or she have a favorite color, or flower?"

"Yes, her favorite color is yellow, and I know she likes this certain flower. I can't remember the name but I'd know it if I saw it."

"My biggest sellers in that color are chrysanthemums, daffodils and, of course, roses. Let me get our flower book to help you find just the right one for your friend."

The cashier walked over to a desk and looked around. "Oh, it's in the office." She turned to Ike. "Be right back."

Ike turned to view the flowers in the glass display. Just then, a high-pitched yelp, followed by the sound of scurrying nails on tile, broke the silence. He caught a glimpse of fur bursting through a doggy door he'd not even noticed.

"Snappy! Bad dog!" The woman who'd been assisting him was hot on his paws. "Snappy! Get back here!"

Ike watched briefly before turning back to the display. People and their dogs. Growing up there were many animals on his grandparents' farm, and the Drakes had owned a collie when the boys were young. The dog had been a member of the family for twelve long years. When their parents offered the chance to get another dog, the boys had turned it down. The loss had been too painful. Except for Warren, none of the brothers had pets to this day.

Turning back to the display, he spotted the flower Audrey loved. At the same time, the saleswoman, breathing heavily, returned to the store. She went inside the office beyond the counter, retrieved the flower book and closed the door on the runaway canine.

"I'm so sorry," she said, still panting for breath. "Wasn't even thinking when I opened the door."

"It's okay. I actually found the flower in your display case." He pointed to a flower holder on the top shelf.

"Oh, the calla lilies. Great choice. I'm not sure I have yellow in stock, but I'll check." She looked at the closed door. "Tell you what. Let's look at bouquets using the calla lily and I'll make sure to get your phone number when I write up the order. If I don't have any yellow ones, I can include those in a design using other yellow flowers."

"Sounds perfect."

"Thank you. I just don't want to chance opening the door again right now while he's still hyped up."

"He's a fast one."

"He is that. Makes it almost impossible to catch him sometimes, but I wouldn't have it any other way. A month or so ago, his ability to run fast saved his life."

"Oh, really."

"Yes, just about gave me a heart attack. Happened right near the corner. A red sports car ran into this cute little black car. I felt so bad. Crushed that thing something awful, and all because she was trying to avoid that disobedient critter. I ran after him for two blocks, but knowing how mad I was, he hid under a Dumpster. By the time I got back to check on that lady, the ambulance had taken her to the hospital. But the EMT told me she'd be okay. I used to never have a problem with him staying inside. Course, I've only had him six months or so. I guess he just realized what the doggy door was for."

Ike hadn't heard a word past *red sports car*. She was talking about his accident. No one had believed Quinn's dog-dodging story. Ike thought she'd been trying to lessen her culpability. But she'd been telling the truth.

"Here I am going on and on while you look like a man with more to do than hear me prattle. Let me show you a couple of examples I think you'd like."

"Did you arrange the bouquets in those display cases?"

"Sure did. I'm the owner. It's just me and a couple of high school students who work a few hours a week."

Ike reached for his wallet and pulled out a business card. "Then I will trust your judgment to create something wonderful."

"I appreciate your confidence." She looked at the card. "Oh, you're a Drake. Your company built the home we bought."

"I hope it is serving you and your family well."

"We're extremely satisfied." She stapled the card to an order form. "What is your budget, Mr. Drake?"

"Whatever you feel is reasonable. Put together something nice. I'll have my secretary call with a delivery address." He reached into his wallet again and pulled out a bill. "Thank you."

"Oh, no, this is probably more than you'll pay for the bouquet."

"You've been extremely helpful. Treat yourself to something nice."

Ike walked back to the office in a different frame of

mind. His father was disappointed, his brothers were angry and he hadn't heard from Quinn about a meeting with Corrigan. But at least one mystery had been solved. There had been a dog at the accident scene. And his name was Snappy.

Chapter 25

The next day, Friday, he got the call he'd been expecting.
"Ike Drake."

"Hey, Ike."

"Hello, Quinn. How are you?"

"Better than you, it sounds. Are things still pretty rough there?"

"It's a difficult time. The entire office went from being swamped with work, busy preparing for a major event—Ten Drake Plaza, and all of a sudden that frenzy is gone, and not with the celebratory ending we all anticipated. So, yes, it's rough. Depressing. And it's my fault."

"I'm sorry, Ike. I feel bad for what's going on in the office. After all, it's partly my fault, too. None of this would have happened if not for me."

"Don't beat yourself up about it. At the end of the day, it was my responsibility to receive the information and process it logically and critically. Follow that up with research and cross-checks. All the things that I do on a regular basis, even for unimportant transactions. I still can't believe how I reacted, or that I reacted. It was probably one of the costliest lessons in history, but I've learned it. And something like that will not happen again."

"For what it's worth, I believe you did the right thing."

Niko walked into Ike's office.

"Look, Quinn, someone just entered my office."

"Okay. I just wanted to know if you're busy tonight, and if not, are you up for a date?"

"You're back in PC."

"Yes."

"I'll call you later."

Ike watched Niko take a seat in one of two chairs that faced his desk. "What's on your mind, brother?"

"I came to check on you."

"Wait a minute. That's my job."

"It's okay for the younger brother to lift the older brother once in a while."

"I appreciate it."

"So how are you holding up?"

"Ah, man. I don't even know. I've analyzed and rationalized to within an inch of my life, and at the end of the day, the result is the same. And that's really all that matters."

"I made a couple discreet inquiries about Global 100, and what Quinn said."

"And?"

"Nothing but positive feedback, the same information on the reports we received. Bernard might walk a fine ethical line, but there was nothing that would corroborate what you shared. And I pulled in some favors, talked with big guns."

"I'm not surprised. This information is known only by the highest echelons of society, and even there, only the ones who are willing to sell their soul for a dollar. This isn't being discussed on the golf course or at private clubs. This is another level. Brother, we're talking murder, starvation, corruption to the core."

"Or so you've been told."

"That's the most aggravating part of all. Well, besides letting go of a few million dollars."

"Hmm."

"I may never be able to find out if what I acted on is true. To go the rest of my life not knowing will eat me up inside."

"You can't let it do that, Ike. We all make mistakes. You don't make many, but being human, it happens. We make money, lose it, make some more."

"This is the biggest loss in the history of our company."

"See, that's where perspective comes in. You can't lose what you've never had. We haven't lost any money. We lost an opportunity to potentially make money. Big difference."

"Man, you are definitely a politician!"

"Hey, I can't help my keen intellect and eloquent speech."

"Can anybody? Because we need to find whoever that is and fly them in!"

"It's good to see you laugh, man. You've got to keep the balance. I hope you're leaving here pretty soon with plans to spend the evening doing something enjoyable."

"Negative."

"What are you doing?"

"What I'm doing right now."

"That's not good. You need a break. Why don't you join me and Monique for dinner? We're going to a dinner theater venue. Should be fun."

"I hope it is, and appreciate the invitation. But I'm going to pass."

Niko stood. "All right. Don't say I didn't try."

Ike stood and came around the desk. "I appreciate your coming by and showing your support. It means a lot."

The brothers hugged. Niko left. Ike resumed working. But not for long. Ten minutes later, his cell phone rang. Quinn. He almost sent the call to voice mail but remembered he was supposed to return her call.

"Ike Drake."

"Whoa, so businesslike. Do you still have someone in your office?"

"No, still working but I've got a few minutes."

"Only a few? I'd love us to meet up once you leave the office."

"Once I leave here, I'll work from home."

"Tonight?"

"Sorry, Quinn. I'm just focused on work right now."

"Come on, Ike. Even the president of the United States takes a vacation, and he's the leader of the free world! We've never had a proper date. You're a great cook and have a beautiful home. But we've never done anything else or gone anywhere."

"This is who I've been from the beginning. I told you up front."

"You told me you liked being at home. You didn't say that's all you'd ever do every day for the rest of your life."

"Maybe it isn't. But that's what I'm going to do tonight." He continued through the huffing of her disgust. "Quinn, I don't mean to sound callous or frustrate you. The week has been intense, and you know why. I have just as much work this weekend. And given that I single-handedly destroyed the deal of a lifetime for the company I run, I'm not in a partying frame of mind."

"Okay. I get it. I guess...we'll talk later."

"If you change your mind and want to spend time with a boring old man, you're more than welcome to stop by."

Ike tried to get back to work, but turning down two invitations in less than thirty minutes had him taking stock of his life. Maybe it was boring and needed to change. After Ten Drake Plaza was rectified, maybe he'd do something about it. But not before.

Something jolted him awake. Ike looked around, rubbed his eyes, looked again. He'd fallen asleep in his office. What time was it? He looked at the clock and was shocked to see it was almost midnight. He'd vaguely remembered laying his head against the chair. Was going to close his eyes for five minutes. That was two hours ago.

Ding.

He wasn't dreaming. That was his doorbell. At this time of night? Ike walked toward the front door, hoping whoever it was didn't have bad news.

"Quinn?"

"That's right," she said, brushing past without an invitation. "You invited me. Remember?"

"That was hours ago."

"Hey, I can't help it if you don't answer your phone."

"You called?"

"Twice."

"I fell asleep. Man, I must have really been out of it." Ike plopped down on the couch and closed his eyes.

"Perfect position for what I have in mind."

"I'm sorry, Quinn. I'm really tired."

Quinn reached for his belt buckle. "No problem. I understand."

"What are you doing?"

"Don't worry about me." She unzipped his pants. "Just raise up a little and I'll be fine."

"Quinn, come on now."

"Are you going to sleep in your clothes? I'm trying to help."

"You're not going to leave me alone, are you?"

"Nope."

He raised up.

She reached into his boxers for the prize inside.

"Sweet, I told you..."

"I know. Just relax. I got this."

She did, and knew exactly what she wanted to do with it, too. She flicked her tongue across the mushroom tip. His shaft twitched. Quinn smiled. Not all of Ike was asleep. She ran her tongue around the rim, up and down his lengthening member.

"Quinn, come on..."

Not as much conviction, she noticed.

"Shh. Just relax."

Long, wet strokes from base to tip. Over and again. As he got harder, longer. Fully aroused. Quinn paused long enough to pull the condom she'd brought from its foil wrapper. She placed a shield on his sword, eased down on it and began to ride.

It wasn't long before Ike joined her.

"I told you I was tired," he murmured as he thrust up into her in that slow, lazy way that drove her crazy.

"You just keep being tired, baby. Just keep…on…right there."

Later, in bed, Quinn listened to the smooth, even sounds of Ike's slumber, thought of how even in his exhaustion he made sure she was satisfied. He was willing to put in the work for what she wanted. There was one thing Ike wanted. Quinn knew what it was. And she was going to put in the work to make sure he got it.

Chapter 26

Quinn whipped into a parking space near a restaurant Phillip Corrigan had assured her she'd enjoy. When'd she'd acted on impulse and included a brief but informative overview of the proposed Ten Drake Plaza building with the thank-you note for the hospitality during her visit, it was simply to underscore what they'd discussed and reinforce the selling points. Basic Business 101.

So receiving his phone call had caught her totally off guard. So much so that afterward she'd phoned Trent, sure that he'd had something to do with what seemed to be his father's genuine interest in doing business with the Drakes. She'd imagined it but had never thought it was actually possible to initiate a negotiation. Yet here she sat, about to dine with an investor.

"Look at me," she spouted, her English accent perfect as she used the visor mirror to freshen up. "I'm a businesswoman, I am."

She exited the car wearing Brenda's dress, the name she'd given the royal blue sheath Maggie had found in her closet. The dress that had inspired that conversation about her mother had been the catalyst for the new level of relationships she now enjoyed. Once inside, she was quickly ushered to a table where Phillip stood to greet her.

"Good evening!" Air kisses and a genuine hug followed before taking their seats. "I hope you weren't waiting long."

"I purposely got here early, wanted to unwind and enjoy a glass of wine. Becky is away visiting her sister. That house gets pretty big and lonely when she's gone."

"In that case, I'm happy to have inspired this meeting. I was surprised but delighted to get your call."

"Probably not half as surprised as I was to get the report you compiled. I must say, I was impressed, young lady. Didn't know you had it in you! And I mean that in a good way."

Quinn laughed. "There's no need to explain. You knew me during the rebel years, when I was a tornado tearing up everything in sight and destroying myself a bit along the way. I guess I'm finally growing up."

"You've grown into a beautiful woman, Quinn. I was rather proud to know that report was your work. Actually, you are what initially made this project of any interest or relevance to me. As I began to look into some of the numbers you provided and talked to a few people, lo and behold, there began to be serious conversation about taking a closer look. That's why you're here."

"I'll be happy to share as much as I know, which isn't much more than what I sent you. A meeting with the Drakes would give those interested all pertinent details."

"Tell me about them. How you came to work for them, first of all, and then whatever you can share. I looked them up online, of course, and found that we actually know some of the same people. But it's always good to get personal opinions."

An impish grin appeared on Quinn's face. "Well, Mr. Corrigan, that story begins with an accident that was blamed on excessive speed by yours truly."

"A total mistake, I'm sure."

"Absolutely and completely."

"There's no way Quinn Taylor would drive a Corvette over the speed limit."

"Exactly."

Her laughter mingled with his. "In truth, I may have been going a tiny bit over the limit, but in my defense, this little doggy ran in front of my car. I swerved to avoid it, and that's when it happened. The car I hit belonged to Ike Drake, the COO of Drake Realty Plus. Unfortunately, it was a vintage Ferrari…"

"Ouch!"

"To say the least, he was not happy. But sitting here now, sharing the story with you, puts the incident in a different light. It could have been destiny introducing the Drakes to their catalyst for a very important sale."

Phillip raised his glass. "Hear, hear."

Later, Quinn walked to her car. But she could have floated just as easily. Had the well-respected, well-connected former banker and financier Phillip Corrigan just agreed to hear more about Ten Drake Plaza from Drake Realty Plus COO Ike Drake Jr.? She wanted to skip, dance, scream, turn cartwheels. But she continued the leisurely yet purposeful walk of a professional woman on the way to her car as if she hadn't just accomplished a goal so daunting that she'd not even set it. Sure, part of the motivation behind visiting the Corrigans had been to discuss Compliance National and the sale of their former headquarters building. But Quinn felt fairly certain that Phillip had done business with Global 100 while he was president of the bank. Given how skittish Trent said he was on that topic, and knowing talk of the bank could bring up those memories, Quinn knew an extended conversation on that topic was no guarantee. But when Phillip mentioned Compliance National, it gave Quinn the opening she needed to casually mention her internship with one of the companies wanting to purchase it. How Phillip would react to this was anyone's guess. Quinn hoped for at least a passing interest in Drake Realty Plus. Phillip had gone above and beyond that expectation. He'd wanted to hear all about her work and how her education had enhanced the experience. What she'd shared with him had led to dinner tonight, and to the news that made her giddy. She could barely contain herself.

There was no scream, but when Quinn was finally in her car, she exclaimed a hearty, "Yes!" Once headed home, her real dilemma began—how to break the news to Ike. Her first choice was to do it in person, but she knew that was out. There was no way she'd be able to sit on this news until back in PC. A text would be much too impersonal, but given their limited communication of late, reaching him by phone was no guarantee. But she had to try. Good news was meant to be shared.

She engaged her Bluetooth and called him.

"Hello, Quinn."

"Ike, I'm glad you answered."

"You thought I wouldn't?"

"I didn't know if you'd be available and I didn't want to leave the reason I'm calling in a voice message."

After a brief pause he said, "What reason is that?"

"To tell you about my meeting with Phillip and his desire to talk to you!"

"Phillip Corrigan?"

"That's the one!"

"How did that happen?"

Quinn told him. The long version. "Even when he suggested we continue the conversation over dinner, there was no guarantee anything would happen as a result. So I didn't want to say a thing until I had a firm commitment of his desire to hear more about Ten Drake Plaza and to meet with you."

"Wow. I don't know what to say."

"Any number of responses would be appropriate—'You're amazing,' 'I'm impressed,' 'You rock,' 'This is a start but you're still on our list,' or maybe just 'thank you.'"

"Thank you."

"You're welcome. I can't wait to hear what happens when you tell your family."

"I don't know, Quinn. Your excitement is contagious. I think you should tell them."

Chapter 27

When Ike asked Quinn to attend the meeting at Drake Realty, Quinn drove back into San Francisco for the perfect outfit. She'd found it at Nordstrom, a classic black suit combining a pencil skirt with a peplum jacket. Velvet pockets with exposed silver zippers added a little Quinn to the conservative design. Understated silver jewelry was an appropriate complement, but the silver tips of her black Louboutin ankle boots revealed a hint of inner brashness that would not conform or be tamed.

The meeting was scheduled for 3:00 p.m. At 2:50, Quinn pulled into the familiar parking lot and went inside. Unlike the first visit, when she argued with the receptionist and was kept waiting outside, she was greeted by name within seconds of stepping to the counter.

"Right this way, Ms. Taylor," said an assistant, one Quinn didn't recognize. "Would you like something to drink?"

"No, thank you. I'm fine." She glanced at her watch. "I would like a quick stop in the ladies' room, though."

"Of course."

Quinn went inside and rechecked her skirt, making sure the slit was perfectly centered. She pulled a Kleenex from the box and dabbed a slight sheen from her face, then flipped her hair for added body, allowing the loose curls to cascade freely down her back. At 2:57, she emerged from the room and continued with the assistant to the conference room.

"Here we are, Ms. Taylor. If you need anything, just buzz up front."

"Thank you." After a deep breath, Quinn squared her shoulders and walked confidently into the room. The chatter just before she entered diminished as each person in the room stopped to watch her entrance.

"Good afternoon, everyone." Her smile was effortless as she made eye contact with those around the table. Seeing Lydia, she waved and followed her hand motion directing her to the head of the long conference table. She felt Ike's eyes on her, could imagine his thoughts, but kept her focus on the matter at hand. This was a huge moment, one that could potentially save Ten Drake Plaza, restore her man's name and reputation, and, perhaps, seal his love. She was not going to mess it up.

Quinn set her purse in the chair, pulled out a five-by-seven note card and remained standing. She forced herself to meet Terrell's curious eyes and Ike Sr.'s slightly amused, slightly impressed ones. Lydia beamed like a proud mom. Warren tried to look neutral, but Quinn could tell he was shocked. Hopefully, their amazement would continue.

"I would like to thank Mr. Drake—Ike—for inviting me to speak with you. I can't begin to do that without pointing out the irony of this occurring. The last person I'd thought would invite me anywhere, ever—" she paused as laughter and comments created a low murmur "—was the man whose prized classic car I destroyed. So it just goes to show how unpredictable life can be.

"If I thought the accident destroyed any chances for my presence in your boardroom, then what happened more recently closed and locked the door. I want you to know that I was devastated at what happened as a result of what I'd shared, information I believed to be true but also understood could be costly. It makes what I'm about to share all the more satisfying. So, thank you again.

"I met Phillip Corrigan almost ten years ago, when I was sixteen. His son, Trent, and I are best friends and he and his wife, Becky, had flown to Switzerland for a visit. It wasn't long before I was just another one of their kids. As you know, my dad, the Honorable Judge Glen Taylor, lives in San Francisco, and during a recent visit I reconnected with Mr. and Mrs. Corrigan, as well. As we caught up on each other's lives, my stint here at Drake Realty came up, and with it, a brief discussion of the proposed Ten Drake Plaza—the old Compliance National building where Mr. Corrigan was president. That, I knew, would be of interest to him. Afterward, along with a thank-you note for their hospitality, I attached a brief overview of what I felt made this such an attractive opportunity. While not getting my hopes up, I wanted desperately to rectify the problems my information had caused."

She pulled out copies of the two-page report and handed them to Lydia, who passed them down the table.

"Last week, Mr. Corrigan contacted me about what I'd sent him. He invited me to dinner. I didn't tell Ike or any of you, because quite frankly I didn't want anything else I said to potentially be untrue. It wasn't my intent to go behind your backs or become an employee by default or anything like that, just so you understand. I put together what you're reading fairly quickly, almost as an afterthought, so I wasn't overly confident that anything would happen. But I am pleased to be able to announce that Mr. Corrigan is indeed interested in a meeting with you, Ike, first of all, and then depending on its outcome, with other members of the company."

She allowed a glance then, and was rewarded with a look so hot it seared her soul. The others around the table were visibly both stunned and impressed as well. Quinn allowed herself a mini inner celebration. The meeting, at least, looked to be a success.

"I would like to pause now and take questions if anyone

has them regarding my meeting with Mr. Corrigan, the report or anything I've discussed."

There were a few questions, but most people who commented said just two words: "Thank you."

Chapter 28

"The second passenger just arrived, Mr. Drake. I'll alert the pilot. We'll be ready to take off shortly."

"Thanks, Stan." Ike left the waiting area and walked toward the hangar entrance. He breathed a sigh of relief, only now willing to admit his fear that she wouldn't show. He reached the car and waved away the company driver. "I've got it, buddy. Thanks a lot."

He opened her car door and helped her out. "Hello, Quinn. Thanks for coming. I'm really glad to see you."

"Your promise of a fun, adventurous two days in Vegas without you doing any work whatsoever, even so much as sending an email or text, was too good of an opportunity to prove you wrong. Because I don't believe you can do it. Ike Drake? All weekend and no work at all? Nope, don't believe that's possible."

"You being here with me right now is proof that everything's possible."

They walked inside the hangar. The plane idled. A maintenance engineer made his final check. Stan, the full-time pilot for the company plane, came from the plane and down the steps. "I assume this is our passenger. Good afternoon."

"Hello."

"If you're ready, we're ready."

"All right then. My luggage is already on the plane. Your clothes are in the Vegas boutiques. I'd say we're ready to go."

The first ten minutes were spent going through the usual

preflight drill. Ike and Quinn settled into their seats. Stan announced they'd reached cruising altitude.

Quinn turned to Ike. "Okay, I'm here. You wanted to talk. So talk."

"I know I've been busy, distracted and unavailable lately. Honestly, it wasn't only because of what happened with Ten Drake Plaza, but also because of my conflicted feelings toward you and how what you shared impacted the company and my family. While there is an undeniable attraction, I began to wonder if that was enough to overcome all that has happened. But the longer I stayed away, the worse I felt. So here you are."

"I went along with what you said earlier but I've missed you, Ike. It wouldn't have taken a bribe to get me here. I've never felt with anyone else the way I do with you. I didn't even think feelings like that existed, except in the movies, maybe, or romance novels. I've allowed myself to begin to believe that maybe, just maybe this is going to be the situation I've always wanted and never had. A situation where I mattered more than the business. That I would be the priority, that it would be you and me no matter what. It may be irrational or premature to think this way, but it's how I feel. I don't know if this will work, either, or whether your family could ever totally welcome me into the fold. I could never stay where I'm not wanted or accepted. Experiencing that as a child caused trauma from which I'm still healing. But I'm here now because it's where I want to be. With you. If not forever, then at least for now."

"I don't know what might happen, either. My dad was impressed with your presentation. Warren appreciated your initiative and willingness to try and help the situation. Terrell was less forthcoming with how he felt. I'd like to think that my family will come to embrace you as I do. I don't do casual relationships. My time is too valuable for that. So it seems there is a decision to be made. Because for this to work we have to be in it together all the way, or not at all."

* * *

When they arrived at the hotel an hour later and entered the room, Ike's comment about true commitment took on new meaning. He'd reserved a two-bedroom suite and, after giving her first choice on the one she wanted, had the bellman deposit his luggage in the smaller room.

He checked his watch and said, "You have thirty minutes to freshen up, change or do whatever you women do in the bathroom that takes so long. But our first reservation is in forty and we can't be late."

Exactly thirty minutes later, Ike knocked on her door. When she opened it, his hand remained where he'd raised it to knock as his eyes took a scenic tour from her hair to her tan lace-up boots and back to her eyes.

"You said to dress casual. Is this too casual?"

He smiled and shook his head. "Sweet, you don't look casual at all. You look delicious. Which is why we probably should leave right now."

They reached the elevator. Ike pushed the button.

"I thought you said we had a reservation."

"We do."

"Then why'd you push the up button?"

"Because that's the direction I want us to travel."

"I browsed the hotel directory. The restaurants are lower level."

"That is correct."

"So where are we—"

Ding.

The elevator door opened to a short, plain hallway with a door on each side and one at the end.

"What's up here?"

Just before Ike opened the door at the end, he turned and told her. "Our ride."

"A helicopter! Cool! I've never ridden in one before."

"Get ready for our first adventure."

Soon, they were in the air. Wearing specially equipped

earphones, they were able to converse easily and listen to the pilot's running commentary on the places they toured: Lake Mead, the Hoover Dam and finally the Grand Canyon, where the helicopter touched down behind a log cabin. It turned out to be a restaurant, where the two enjoyed a simple but yummy lunch of steak and salad before leaving by taxi for the next item on Ike's agenda.

One look at the sign and Quinn squealed. "We're going horseback riding!"

Indeed they were. Ike had arranged a tour for just the two of them. They explored ancient Native American trails, viewed original rock art created around 1300 AD and watched the sun go down on the Grand Canyon floor.

Back in Las Vegas they changed for a more formal dinner at Picasso, fine French- and Spanish-inspired cuisine in a room boasting originals of the famous artist's work. They both agreed that no show could compare to seeing Michael Jackson live, but still they enjoyed One, the Cirque du Soleil show based on his music. Capping off this first day was dancing at one of the strip's hottest nightclubs before Ike suggested after-dinner drinks in their room.

"I can't believe you!" Quinn declared as they entered the suite. "Those dance moves. And for an hour! You broke out your inner party boy."

"I do that every five years or so."

"Ha!"

"Sit right there. I'll make our drinks."

Quinn sat down, pulled off her four-inch stilettos and began to massage her feet.

Ike noticed. "I'll do that for you. Give me a minute."

He returned with a tray bearing two bottles of sparkling water, two snifters of Grand Marnier and a small velvet bag.

"What's this?"

"I don't know," Ike replied, his eyes sparkling. "Why don't you look inside and find out?"

Quinn's hands shook slightly as she opened the bag,

reached inside and pulled out a silver box. "This is beautiful. Is this real silver?"

Ike shook his head. "It's platinum."

"This is platinum?" Ike nodded. "Thank you, babe. It's beautiful, but…what do I do with it?"

"You open it, silly."

"Oh! It's so pretty I thought the box was the gift." She turned the box, found a small indentation and lifted the lid. "Ahh, isn't this adorable!"

It was a platinum necklace, stunningly displayed against a black velvet lining. Diamonds created the dog-shaped pendant's fur, with heart-shaped black diamonds as eyes.

"I remember you being very adamant about a dog running in front of your car the day you hit me. I saw that while flipping through a magazine and thought it a perfect apology token."

"I was adamant because there was a dog! I swear on my life, Ike. I only saw it for seconds before it disappeared under my car, or so I thought. Why else would I have come in your lane?"

"I don't know." He shrugged. "Maybe it was an ingenious way to meet me."

Quinn jumped up. "Are you serious? You think I'd wreck my car to meet somebody? No. I did it to avoid hitting a dog. Argh!" she continued, her rant ratcheting up. "I don't know where it came from. I don't know where it went. But it was there! And it drives me crazy that nobody saw it but me. But that doesn't take away from the fact that a dog ran in front of my car that day. There. Was. A. Dog!"

"I know."

"I wish I could find it. I'd give the owner a piece of my—what did you just say?"

Ike chuckled. "I said there was a dog."

"You believe me?"

"I do."

"What changed your mind?"

He told her about his experience at the florist shop. "The second she said accident and red car, I knew she was talking about us."

Quinn dropped to the couch in dramatic relief. "Thank the heavens!" She sat up. "I'm going to that shop first thing Monday morning. I'm going to take pictures to give to the court and prove I was not lying. They might even drop my case. Then you'll owe me the money I paid you."

"If that happens, being able to sit here and witness your reaction would make it totally worth it."

"Here, put it on me."

"Turn around." She did and raised her hair. "So…did you enjoy yourself today?"

"Immensely."

She turned and hugged him. "It was the most fun I've had in a while. Thank you."

"I'm going to bed," he said with a yawn. He stood up. "You might want to try and get some sleep as well. Our next adventure is first thing in the morning, at eight o'clock sharp." He kissed her forehead. "Good night, sweet."

Quinn went into her bedroom. She didn't stay long. After taking off everything except the diamond doggy, she crossed the living room to his door, raised her hand to knock and then, instead, slowly turned the knob and opened the door.

"Ike?"

He turned. Stopped. Stared. Didn't move.

"I didn't want to wait, and wondered if there was any chance we could start our next adventure right now."

He smiled broadly, walking toward her as he replied, "I'd hate to keep a lady waiting."

They set off on an adventure that lasted until dawn.

Chapter 29

It happened sooner than he'd expected, but Ike wasn't complaining. Today, he'd have lunch with Phillip Corrigan in the privacy of the Drakes' San Francisco home. That they were discussing Ten Drake Plaza was only one reason. Ike also planned to broach the sensitive subject that was Global 100. Had he gone off half-cocked when he confronted Bernard? Or had he followed his gut and revealed an ugly truth? Ike needed to know.

He'd dressed to impress—custom navy suit, pin-striped shirt, gold cuff links and tie pin, bespoke shoes—flawless. He walked around the room and was satisfied with its appearance. The housekeeper had done a stellar job. There wasn't one speck of dust or a thing out of place. The dining table held a posh setting for two with Baccarat goblets and Royal Crown Derby dinnerware. Mouthwatering aromas escaped the kitchen as a two-Michelin-star chef prepared side dishes to accompany organic Chateaubriand.

The meeting was set for one o'clock. The doorbell rang at 12:59. A person mindful of the value of time was Ike's kind of guy.

"Phillip! Come right in."

"Ike!" Phillip stepped through the door and shook Ike's outstretched hand. "It's a pleasure to finally meet you in person."

"The pleasure is mine, sir."

Phillip walked in, admiring the architecture and the smartly appointed decor. "Nice place you have here."

"Thank you. It gives us the privacy we need to speak freely. This way, please. Lunch is ready to be served."

During the soup and salad courses, Ike and Phillip learned a bit more about each other before recapping the key points from earlier phone conversations. Both agreed that buying the Compliance National building was a smart choice. By the time the entrée arrived, Phillip's interest was clear. Ike knew he'd baited the hook well and had his catch on the line.

"Let me ask a question, Ike. I know you're looking for investors, but would you guys give any consideration to partnering in the ownership?"

"Traditionally, that is not a path we've chosen, for many reasons. That's what made the offer from Global 100 such an agreeable one. They weren't interested in owning the building, only profiting from it. Any time after their investment was recouped, they could walk away. However, my philosophy is to put all options on the table and to remain open while they're discussed." After a brief follow-up discussion, Ike said, "Now, Mr. Corrigan, I have a question for you."

"Go right ahead."

"I understand you've done business with Global 100."

There was an immediate shift in Phillip's demeanor. "I have."

"Our business arrangement with Global 100 collapsed because of disturbing news I heard regarding their business practices. Are you familiar with any of them?"

"Ike, I understand you asking the question, and yes, I did business with Global in the past, as I did with hundreds of businesses across the country and around the world. I'm sure you can understand that all the information we shared or that I learned as result is confidential."

"Absolutely. I also know that discussing this company in particular is sensitive, and potentially dangerous. What I heard involves high-level individuals with lots of power and resources. The stories I heard were of corruption and brutal takeovers, theft and deceit, invisible partners and blood money."

He looked directly into Phillip's eyes as he spoke. Watched his body language. Noticed a pale shade of red begin to creep up from his neck.

"I heard all of that, Mr. Corrigan, and without consulting my family made the decision to research the information, completely prepared to walk away from what we believe will be a very lucrative situation rather than jeopardize the Drake name or the integrity that we stand for. So let me ask a different question. What do you think of the decision I made?"

The slightest of smiles crossed Phillip's face. "Your research is sound and your decision spot-on."

The look in Phillip's eyes further conveyed that what Quinn had told him was true.

"You're a fine man, Ike, from a great family. I'd be proud to partner with you in business, and to call you a friend. I've spoken with a few associates who I knew would be interested in the project. They would like to meet with you as well as others from your executive committee to see how we can come together and get this deal done."

"I'm glad to hear that, sir. It's good news indeed." Ike picked up a wine-filled goblet. "To business and friendship."

Phillip raised his glass. "Indeed."

That evening, the Drake family gathered in one of Paradise Cove's private dining rooms, where Ike announced what had taken place in San Francisco. He'd invited Quinn, who stood by his side.

"In closing, I'd like to recognize the lady beside me." He turned to her. "Quinn, while the manner in which it happened caused a minor earthquake in Paradise Cove, and in the Drake family—" he paused as people laughed "—the information you learned and passed on kept us from making an unholy alliance. Your relationship with Phillip Corrigan and the initiative you showed in presenting our plan to him helped secure a new avenue for funding and success. I'd like to publicly thank you for that and to acknowledge that you are the most unique, aggravating, unpredictable, intelligent and beautiful woman I've ever met."

As the room applauded, Ike Sr. stood and walked to the front of the room. He placed a hand on Ike's shoulder.

"When I heard that this man, my oldest son, had gone to our investor and in effect ruined the biggest deal we'd ever handled, I was madder than a teetotaler locked in a liquor store. I was furious! And I was so disappointed. He tried to explain his reasoning, how the feeling in his gut made him do what he did because he felt there was no time to waste. At the time, I forgot all about the fact that following your gut is one of the first lessons I taught him. There have been many others. He's mastered them all. He's a better businessman than I am. A more upstanding human being has never walked the earth.

"He'll hear these words several times before this night is over. But I'm going to be the first one to say them. Son, I'm sorry for how I reacted, and couldn't be prouder."

Ike was too choked up to speak. He nodded and accepted his father's hug. Jennifer left her chair to hug him as well. Soon, a circle of Drakes surrounded the eldest son to apologize, congratulate and share their love.

Quinn stood to the side, her eyes shining with tears and pride. Jennifer looked up and noticed.

"Come on over and join the circle, Quinn Taylor. You're part of our family, too."

Chapter 30

Quinn stared at herself in the mirror, conflicting emotions warring within her that jumbled her nerves and made it hard to breathe. She'd been to a Drake family function, but the casual ranch atmosphere was totally different from the Thanksgiving plans that Jennifer had described. Her dad and Viviana were coming, which further shook her nerves. He'd met Ike Drake, Sr., but how would her reserved dad and stepmother get along with Ike and his boisterous family?

She was saddened that even with the turnaround of the business deal, her relationship status with Ike still felt tentative. Granted, he'd been overwhelmed with work and meetings, and said it wasn't personal—it was Jennifer, not Ike, who'd invited the Taylor family to this affair. Still, she was grateful, because for the first time she'd spend the holiday with a family that seemed to truly love and enjoy having each other around.

A glance at the clock told Quinn there was no more time to hide out in her room. It was time to join the family downstairs and head over to the Drakes'.

When she came down the stairs, Glen stood and held out his arms. "You look beautiful, honey."

"Thanks, Dad."

"He's right, Quinn. You look absolutely stunning. That color adores you."

"Thank you, Viviana. You look beautiful."

Quinn turned as her grandmother came out of the kitchen. "Now there's the real star!"

Maggie's eyes twinkled as she preened. "Vanity is unseemly, but I think I look quite nice."

"Mom, Quinn, baby, are we ready to go?"

Everyone answered in the affirmative and within minutes, they were out the door. Quinn sat in the back of the limo taking them to Golden Gates wondering if this dinner would turn out to be her bon voyage.

Ike walked outside to where Thanksgiving dinner would be held, moved from the dining room by the increased guest count. He eyed the festive decorations—blue and yellow, as he'd requested. He hadn't always been the most astute when it came to celebrations and making the day special, but he figured one was never too old to step up their game.

Jennifer approached him. "Does it meet with your approval?"

Ike squeezed her shoulders and planted a kiss on her forehead. "More than that, but I'm not surprised. It looks stunning. And so do you."

"I was just about to say the same thing about you. Terrell and Niko are the Drake men most known for their style, but I like this casual sophistication that you've sported as of late. Dating Quinn at least motivated you to modernize your wardrobe. Is she the reason behind all this as well?"

Jennifer swept her hand across the patio, an area elegantly draped with light blue, pale yellow and white silk panels. The stark white tablecloths boasted blue runners and yellow linen napkins clasped in gold rings. At various times, and especially when the wind blew, delicate hints of jasmine would brush across the nostril, wafting from the surrounding vases that also boasted lilies, irises, hydrangea and blue orchids. Sterling silver serving trays lined the back wall and on the other side of the pool, far enough so as not to intrude but close enough for atmosphere, a three-piece jazz band spoke quietly among themselves as they set up their equipment.

"Why would you say that? We always decorate the patio for special occasions."

"Yes, we do, but I don't normally have your input, let alone your help."

"Just wanted to show off another of my exceptional skills."

Jennifer shook her head. Her children might lack many things, but confidence was not one of them. "Terrell and Aliyah are on their way and her family is also due to arrive any minute. Let me check on things." She kissed his cheek and walked away. Ike took one last look around and went upstairs to change.

Ten minutes later, Quinn and her family followed tastefully crafted signs that led to the dining area. Ike was there to greet them as they came through the side door that opened to the backyard. Four people walked through the gate, but Quinn was the only one he saw. She looked angelic, dressed more modestly than he'd ever seen her outside work. The indigo-colored sweater-like dress brought out the yellow tones in her skin. With hair pulled into a high ponytail, sultry eye shadow and Grecian-styled sandals, she resembled a bronze goddess plucked from the pages of a fairy tale. How could he ever have suggested it was over between them? In this moment, Ike came to one very clear realization. He was a fool.

"You look…magnificent. I love the color of the dress. It matches today's decor."

"Thank you," Quinn replied softly, her expression unreadable, before quickly turning toward her father. "Dad, I think you've met Ike Drake. Ike, this is my dad, Glen Taylor."

"Nice to meet you, sir." Ike initiated a firm handshake. "We've crossed paths, but it's been a while."

"I remember you," Glen replied. "But I've had more dealings with your father."

Glen introduced his wife and then Quinn reached for her

grandmother's hand. "Of course you know my grandmother, Maggie Newman. Grandmother, this is Ike."

"A pleasure to see you again, Mrs. Newman. You are looking as beautiful as ever."

"Why thank you, young man. You're looking quite dapper yourself." She looked between him and Quinn. "You two make a wonderful couple." She leaned in and added in a whisper, "And you'll make pretty babies."

Quinn's eyes widened at the unexpected comment. It was an awkward moment for them both, which Ike covered by directing them to the patio area and over to Jennifer and Ike Sr. Knowing that another opportunity for privacy was hours away, he reached for Quinn's hand.

"Come with me."

Her eyes questioned him but she didn't hesitate. They walked through the patio doors, through the great room where more guests mingled and into a sitting room lined with fine art. He closed the door and pulled her into his arms.

"It's good to see you."

After a moment's hesitation, Quinn returned his embrace. "It's good to see you, too."

He stepped back. "In another ten or fifteen minutes, it's going to be pretty crazy out there."

"How many are coming?"

"Forty."

"Wow, okay. That's a lot of guests."

"I figured to grab a private moment with you while I could." She nodded. "How are you doing?"

"I'm okay. You?"

"I'm getting there. Still busy preparing documentation for Phillip and the potential investors he's gathered, but I've tried to get more rest. I miss you."

"I miss you, too, Ike."

"Sorry I've been so busy."

She waited to see if he'd say more, invite her to do something later—anything to make her feel like more than just a friend. When that didn't happen, she stood on tiptoe and kissed his lips. "I probably should get back, socialize. Thanks again for inviting us. It's nice to share Thanksgiving with a big family like the Drakes."

"Oh, my family is what makes it nice."

"Yeah, the Drake family. And you're a part of that."

They parted, but fifteen minutes later were together again as Jennifer had seated them side by side. The afternoon was lively. The band played, the wine flowed, servers made sure that the plates were kept full. That everyone was having a great time was evident, none more than the Drakes, who teased and joked the entire time. The afternoon had been so lively and filled with boisterous conversation, that when Ike walked to the front and requested silence, the effect was as if a loud stereo had been turned off. A slight humming in the ear could still be heard.

"As many of you know, this has been a busy year for Drake Realty. Which means it's been a busy year for me. But my grandfather Walter over there told his grandchildren time and again that hard work pays off. Nothing good comes easy, he'd say. Anything worth having is worth working for. Hard work never killed anyone. Sacrifice over selfishness. I could go on and on with quotes I heard from Grandpa."

"You could but you shouldn't!" Terrell yelled. The audience cracked up.

"This from the man who could talk a fat person into a skeleton." The laughter got louder. "All right, I got the point. But I said all of that to say that those lessons became even clearer this year, and not just as it refers to business. But personally, too.

"A couple months ago, I was in an accident." Various comments were heard throughout.

Quinn's brow creased as she prayed he didn't call her out. What in the heck did that have to do with the building in San Francisco?

"I'm okay. Couldn't say the same about my car at the time. But it's being restored as well. I was hit by a woman who reminds me of my sister London. She was driving wildly, reckless…"

Quinn slid down a bit in her seat and wished she could go under the table. If he called her out…

"Her name is Quinn Taylor, and she'd just moved here not long before."

Quinn's face grew warm as his family and the few others who knew her all looked in her direction. A low murmur began among those who didn't.

"I was furious. Demanded punishment in addition to the fine. But it turns out, I got punished, too. You see, the judge ordered Quinn to do an unusual type of community service." He put air quotes around those two words. "He ordered her to work with me at Drake Realty."

The buzz grew.

"Exactly. As you can imagine, I was not happy, and neither was she. It was like oil and water, and not only are those two solutions hard to mix, we didn't even want to mix. And then something crazy happened." Ike looked directly at Quinn. "I fell in love with her."

Her quick intake of breath was the only reaction. Other than that she was frozen with shock.

"I told myself that it was ridiculous. Who falls in love after just one month? Me, that's who. Which is why I'm going to ask Quinn if you'll please come here, sweetheart."

It seemed the longest time before she slowly rose and walked toward him as people clapped. When she reached him, he held her hand.

"I never thought I'd say this, but being in that accident was the best thing that ever happened to me." He reached into his pocket, pulled out a box and got on his knee. "Quinn Taylor, would you do me the honor of becoming Mrs. Drake? Will you marry me?"

She nodded as he stood. Her yes was swallowed in his

kiss. Her hands shook as he placed on her finger a ring with the most beautiful stone she'd ever seen. It was a sapphire, but not the kind sold in mall jewelry stores. Later, by reading the origin and authenticity certificate she'd learn that it was a fairly rare ten-carat untreated Burmese stone mined in Israel, surrounded by pink diamonds and set in platinum. Quinn would also learn that Ike had approached her grandmother for advice on the type of ring he should buy. Her grandmother knew her better than anyone. Sapphire was the perfect choice.

Of successful couples, those with two polar opposites make up a very small fraction. But the odds don't matter when the love is sealed with a sapphire attraction.

* * * * *